WE'LL ALWAYS HAVE SANTORINI

BY
DANIELLE FLUEHR

THIS BOOK IS FOR
George and Veronica,
Evie and Graham,
And Jed.
Because sometimes it only takes a moment to
know someone will be in your life forever.

A special thank you to Jed, Editor-in-Chief.
Megan, Seth, Joanne, Joe, and Will for the inspiration.

ONE

Anna slipped off the stilettos. After being in heels all day, she couldn't bear wearing another pair, even for a date night with Nick. As she thought about Nick coming home she zipped up her black ankle boots. He would finally be back after three weeks away scouting out a location for his newest project. As a T.V. Producer and showrunner, Nick Whittaker would accompany his team to find the perfect place for each one of the reality shows he co-created. His flight should have landed twenty minutes ago.

Anna's phone buzzed as she adjusted her black lace bra under her semi-sheer blouse and smoothed the shirt over her black denim-clad hips. She picked up her phone and looked at the screen before answering. Seeing the call was from Nick, her heartbeat quickened in anticipation of their reunion. Anna hoped it wasn't another delayed flight. It seemed like he rarely arrived home as expected.

Anna hesitated as she held the phone to her ear.

"Hey, Nick. Are you on your way from the airport?"

"Hey, Babe. I couldn't make it out today," Nick told her, apologetically. "We got held up and couldn't get to the airport in time. I'll be on the first flight in the morning."

Anna took a deep breath. Nothing surprised her much anymore when it came to Nick's schedule. Exhaling, she replied, "Do you want me to pick you up tomorrow?"

"No, I'll take a cab."

"Ok. I'll have-"

"I've gotta go, Steven's calling on the other line. I'll see you tomorrow." Nick ended the call with Anna to speak with Steven, Nick's co-producer. Not the first time she's been put aside for one of Steven's calls.

Anna pressed the end button and tossed the phone onto the bed. She began pulling out the pins holding her mahogany hair in a low chignon. She tried to remember when their last date had been. She shook out her hair and paused staring at the wall. She couldn't recall their last date night. Thinking back over the past few months she thought, *Did we go out Easter weekend?* She let out a frustrated *"UGH!" There is no date night, again.* This was the third time in two months they were supposed to have a night out, just the two of them, no work interruptions. But as usual, work interrupted. Again.

Still dressed, ready to go out, she pondered what to do. *I'll call Lauren and Beth, see if either of them can hang out tonight.* It was approaching six o'clock on a Friday evening, so there was a chance her two closest friends already had dinner plans.

Anna reached both of their voicemails and left a brief message for each. "Nick's delayed until tomorrow. I'll probably head to W.G.'s for some takeout. If you get this, let me know if you want to come over for a glass of wine." Figures, her two single friends are probably on hot dates. Married Anna is alone tonight.

Anna grabbed her purse and headed out the side door of their massive cream-colored stucco home. Anna and Nick had purchased the renovated 1920s house six months before their wedding. Anna loved the vintage charm of the Tudor-style mixed with the newly incorporated contemporary luxuries, like heated floors, marble finishes, and updated technology, modernizing the home to the twenty-first century. The five bedroom, six-thousand square feet house was more space than Anna knew what to do with, but Nick promised she would regret going smaller.

She looked down the path leading to the driveway and at the manicured lawn. The property was tucked away just enough so neighbors could wave but not close enough to actually engage in conversation. Anna wondered if all the travel Nick did for work, and her own busy schedule were worth the limited time they had together. For what? A big empty house to come home to after hours of staring at a computer screen? She knew Nick loved what he did, and she enjoyed her work, but what sense did it make if they didn't get to spend time together.

They had talked early on, while dating, that they

would eventually start a family. When they had purchased the gigantic house, Nick insisted they would need the extra bedrooms for their future children. That was three and half years ago. They had been too busy building their careers since. Now, at thirty-three years old, Anna felt like maybe it was time to start the baby conversation, but she and Nick saw less and less of each other. When Nick wasn't traveling, he worked obscene hours writing and developing his show ideas, hiring his production team, schmoozing with executives- the typical *stuff* people do in his business. Anna's job, as an I.T. director for a software company, kept her busy as well. Anytime Nick was able to be home at a reasonable hour, Anna would be stuck at the office, solving a programming issue or out late at a client dinner. How could they start a family if no one was around to raise it?

Anna pushed her thoughts aside, sinking into the drivers seat of her dark gray Audi TT convertible and drove the two miles to Mrs. Winston's Green Grocery, her favorite place for a quick meal or smoothie. In the suburb of Santa Monica, traffic wasn't as heinous as L.A. traffic. Anna pulled into a parking space and headed into the grocery. She selected her usual salad toppings from the salad bar and then ordered a berry smoothie.

As she waited for her order, she looked around at the other patrons in line. A middle-aged woman in a gray-striped suit stood staring at her phone screen while a silver-haired gentleman wearing a tan cardigan was engrossed in a Dan Brown novel. There was a woman who looked close to Anna's age in yoga pants with an infant sleeping in its stroller. Anna felt a yearning to view what she imagined was a plump cherub nestled under the creamy, soft, lamb-covered blanket. Next, Anna's eyes stopped on an Adonis in an untucked white button-down with faded jeans. His dirty blonde hair was clean-cut in the back but had the kind of length on top you could run your hands through. And he did just that as he looked over at Anna and caught her eye. Her cheeks flamed when she was found staring. Then he spoke.

"Anna Clarke, I'd recognize you anywhere. How are you?" he asked in a friendly tone.

Suddenly, familiarity settled in. She was staring at her older brother's *extremely* attractive friend from college, Mark Williams. They had only met a dozen times or so when Josh would bring Mark home during school breaks or summer vacations. As a teenager, and then as a young adult, Anna's heart always skipped a beat when Mark visited. By the time her brother graduated and moved to North Carolina, she was graduated from Loyola Chicago, moved out to California, and hadn't thought about Mark...much. It had to have been 10 years since she last saw him. The last she had heard, he was living in Seattle, working at a law firm.

She looked into his hazel eyes, "Hey, oh my god, I didn't recognize you." Frazzled, she said, "What are you doing here?"

"Picking up dinner," he teased, knowing that wasn't what she was really asking. "I assume like most people here."

She smiled and ducked her head as she asked, "I mean, why are you in Santa Monica?" She looked up into his eyes adding, "I thought you were living in Seattle."

"Ah, I was. Now I live here." He spread his hands, palms to the sky, emphasizing 'here.' "Well, not *here*," referring to Mrs. WG's store, "but in Santa Monica. I actually just moved into a place last week. I told Josh about a month ago when I got the offer from the office in L.A. He actually told me you live in Santa Monica, and I should look you up."

Anna hadn't talked to her brother since they were all home for the holidays last December, save for a few texts now and then each month. It was May now. "Well, now you found me, even if accidentally. Welcome to the neighborhood." Her order was called, so she took the smoothie off the counter.

Mark looked at her dinner for one and asked, "Do you have plans tonight?" He hadn't meant to intrude on her evening, but she looked just as beautiful as he remembered. All those years ago, he couldn't help noticing his friend's sister, only two years younger, during visits to the Clarke home. Her long dark hair settled in waves around her shoulders, and her chocolate eyes looked up at him under thick lashes.

"Actually, I'm just heading home." Her phone buzzed with a text message from Bethany. "That's my friend, Beth, messaging me back. I was planning some girl time for tonight."

She thought she saw disappointment cross his features briefly before he smiled and said, "Maybe another time then. Let me give you my number." Mark took Anna's dinner to free her hands and waited for her to add him to her phone. Handing her food back, he said: "Let me get yours." Anna gave him her number and wondered if she should mention she had a husband. Mark had called her by her maiden name, and she hadn't thought to correct him. Anna was just so stunned to see him. Before she could say anything, Mark grabbed his own order off the counter and said, "I'm glad I ran into you." He leaned in, giving Anna a one-armed hug. "I'll be in touch." He let her go, turned, and headed towards the registers. Anna waited a beat, taking in the spicy sent of Mark, and then followed. Mark waived another goodbye as he exited the grocery.

Anna slowly walked out to her car, wondering what had just happened. It was innocent enough, but she felt a strange lightness in her chest. It was a familiar sensation that Anna usually associated with Nick's arrivals home after being away. She hadn't had such strong feelings of anticipation with anyone else in a long time.

Seated inside her car, she read the text from Bethany.

I'm out with Drew. Let me know if tomorrow night works. Miss you.

She'd have to see if her date night with Nick would happen tomorrow night instead. Anna sighed deeply and texted back: *Have fun. I'll let you know.*

Arriving back home, she placed her keys and phone

on the table in the entryway. She brought her dinner to the marble kitchen island, deciding to eat while she checked e-mail. After clearing her dishes, she poured a glass of wine and carried it upstairs to undress. She decided she would take a bath and unwind until she heard from Lauren. She ran back downstairs in her underwear to grab her phone and saw she had missed two text messages. The first was from Lauren, apologizing that she couldn't come over. She was getting over a nasty cold and would hopefully be well soon. The second was from Mark Williams. Anna stared at the message.

Do you have plans for tomorrow afternoon? I'd love to pick your brain about the area.

Ok, this was utterly innocuous. Anna texted back: *I won't know my schedule until late morning, can I let you know then?*

Why didn't she just say her husband was returning home and she'd be with him all weekend? Because the truth was she didn't know if she would be with Nick all weekend. She wouldn't know until morning when he got home and confirmed if he had to work. So she left it at that and brought the phone with her upstairs. As she removed the black lace bra, she had bought specially for Nick's homecoming, her phone buzzed with a message from Mark.

No problem. I'll wait to hear from you. Have a good night with the girls.

Anna didn't bother to tell him there wasn't a girls' night - just her, a hot bath, and a glass of Gavi di Gavi. She left her phone on her nightstand and headed to the tub.

TWO

Anna opened her eyes and looked at the clock on her nightstand. Nine after six in the morning. Even without setting her alarm, she woke at roughly the same time each morning. Forget about sleeping in. Her phone blinked with a notification. She read the text message waiting:

Should be home by 12:30pm depending on baggage claim and taxi, 1:30pm at the latest if I have to stop at the office.

Nick sent it at five-fifty, ready for an early morning flight from Vancouver. He hated that he had to travel so much for work, and didn't want Anna to have to wait for him, so he had added: *Feel free to make lunch plans, I'll make it up to you tonight.*

Anna thought about that and decided at nine, a more reasonable hour, she would text Mark and take him up on his offer to meet for lunch. She had a sneaking suspicion that if Nick were already mentioning dinner plans, he would end up stopping at the office and get home later in the afternoon.

Recently it seemed that Nick rarely had free weekends anymore. They've always had busy schedules but after they spent Christmas in New England with Anna's family, Nick's schedule ramped up right after the New Year. It felt decadent to have had those few days with no schedule, waking late in her parents guest room, helping her mom prepare meals while the men showed off splitting wood. Warmth filled Anna as she recalled trying to be quiet in the old four-poster bed with Nick, keeping each other warm on those below freezing nights. But as soon as they landed in LA, Nick was on the phone with Steven back to business. She became sullen at the memory of watching Nick leave for the office on Saturdays or close himself in his home office Sunday mornings.

Anna slipped a silk robe over her camisole and pajama bottoms, and headed downstairs to make a cup of coffee. *Wait a second,* she thought, *why not see if Mark can meet for coffee this morning, then she would still be home by the time Nick arrived? Then again, maybe Mark had morning plans, and that's why he specifically asked about the afternoon. Hmmm, what to do?* Well, as Anna's father always told her, 'It never hurts to ask. The worst is they say no and you're no worse off.' After brewing a cup of coffee--it was early, and she could always order decaf later—then flipping through some travel magazines Nick left lying around, Anna went back up to her closet. Her mood brightened having a plan of attack. She decided on her outfit for the morning, then checked the time. Six fifty-eight a.m. This was going to be a long morning.

She spent a full thirty minutes showering and dressing, then headed back downstairs to make a bowl of oatmeal. As she prepared the oats, Anna eyed the magazines she had left on the kitchen island where she had her morning cup of coffee. The front cover displayed a beautiful view of the Aegean Sea from one of the Greek Islands. She wasn't sure which island, but could identify the white landscape dotted with blue-domes that are signature to Greece. Nick always seemed to pick out amazing locations for his reality shows. With such bizarre themes, the sites must be idyllic for the participants to agree. Looking at the serene picture again, a thought crossed Anna's mind. Maybe she and Nick needed a vacation. Somewhere with amazing views and fruity drinks. No work, just the two of them for a few days.

Her insides warmed at the idea of spending time alone with Nick. It had been too long since they had that, and too short a marriage to feel so isolated. Maybe it would feel normal to spend so much time apart when they were old, and the sex was no longer smoldering. Ha! What sex? Anna couldn't remember the last time they had sex since Christmas break. She knows they have, it's not like they haven't seen each other over the previous months. But they certainly haven't had any real alone time to just be together. She was starting to feel disconnected from Nick. Sometimes, with all his "babe" talk, she felt like he was schmoozing her like he did with his business associates. Anna went from feeling comforted by the idea of a vacation to angry at Nick's lack of trying to make time for her. Was she the only one feeling this way? Didn't he want more time with her? She huffed out air, trying for calm. She didn't know for sure if he would stop at the office rather than come straight home. She really needed to stop jumping to conclusions.

One thing was sure; it was time to message Mark. Anna wanted to call him, knowing that a real conversation is better than always communicating through text messages, but given that it was barely past eight a.m. on a Saturday, she didn't want to risk waking him.

Anna typed out: *Sorry to message so early. Will meeting for coffee work for you, rather than lunch?*

Fifteen excruciating minutes later her phone buzzed with:

Name the place.

Anna responded with a local favorite.

Philz Coffee on Santa Monica BLVD. Do you know it?

After learning Mark knew the location but hadn't been, they agreed to meet in half an hour. Anna looked herself over in the full-length mirror in her bedroom. She decided to lightly line her eyes and add lip balm. She wanted to keep things simple for a breakfast date. Not a date. A meeting. A breakfast meeting with an old acquaintance. She had chosen to wear a pair of faded blue jeans and a light-weight, cream-colored cashmere sweater that contrasted nicely with her dark hair and features. She slipped on a pair of trainers and grabbed her satchel. Throwing her phone inside her oversized bag, she headed out of the house and on her way to meet Mark.

She was looking forward to catching up with him. It had been a long time since she thought about him. Her fondest memories were hanging at the beach with him and Josh, pretending to read while stealing glances at his shirtless, tanned body. Mark and Josh always included her when she wasn't working her summer job at the local coffee shop. Sometimes they would stop in to get iced coffees before heading off on their next adventure, which they would describe to her in detail late at night when they would be in the house together again. She wasn't sure if Josh was oblivious to her crush on his best friend, or he was just being kind to his little sister. Either way, she was grateful he never needled her about it. And nothing ever came of it, anyway.

It was seven minutes before nine when Anna walked into Philz Coffee. The line was long, as usual. Anna scanned the room, looking for Mark. Not seeing him yet, she decided to join the queue assuming he'd arrive well before she would be at the counter to order. Anna kept an eye on the door as customers entered and exited. Barely three minutes had passed when she saw Mark through the glass façade. He was most definitely eye candy. Several people turned their heads to look as he entered, wearing an olive green long-sleeved tee with a pair of grey cargo pants. Anna noticed the green of the shirt brought out gold flecks in his hazel eyes as he scanned the room. She also noticed how nicely his shirt clung to his chest and biceps. Mark made his way through the throng of people crowding the doorway; his six-foot two-inch frame placed his eyes just above the onlookers' heads. Catching sight of Anna, he weaved through the twisting line to join her.

"Hey, popular spot here," Mark said, leaning in to give Anna a hug. "This is really great, only a couple of blocks from the beach." Mark inhaled her coconut shampoo as he gently squeezed her.

Anna accepted the hug, placing one hand on his torso as his arms engulfed her. Mark's lips brushed her cheek as they both pulled away. Her skin tingled after the warmth of the embrace. Smiling up at him, she said, "We can take a walk with our coffee if it's too noisy in here to talk."

After Anna ordered a decaffeinated coffee and Mark ordered a mojito iced-coffee, the specialty, Mark attempted to pay for their drinks. "Nope, I've got this," Anna said. "I changed the plan and asked you to meet for coffee. It's the least I can do to welcome you to town."

Mark knew better than to argue, so he simply thanked Anna. "Next one is on me," he told her firmly.

After Anna put her wallet back in her bag, they found a table to sit and wait. "By the way," she started after they were seated, "I needed to meet earlier because Nick gets home this afternoon. We got married three years ago." It felt good to get it out there.

Mark cleared his throat. "Yeah, I did, in fact, hear that from Josh some time ago. I also couldn't help noticing your left hand had a rock the size of Gibraltar."

"Ha Ha. I like to think that my ring is actually tasteful compared to all the gaudiness this town produces," Anna retorted. She looked down at the carat and a half center stone with the slim band of diamonds flanking each side of the gem. She had a simple platinum band as her wedding ring. "Don't get me wrong, I love it here, but with Nick working in television, there is a lot of the 'keeping up with the Spielbergs.' I like to think I don't get caught up in all of that. I simply try to enjoy the experiences of living out here, being so close to the beach."

"I'm sure you live in a shack," Mark teased her.

Changing the subject, she said, "Our drinks are up. Shall we walk?"

On the walk down to the beach, they talked about some of Mark's more interesting cases and the bungalow he was renting. He asked questions about restaurants and places worth seeing 'as a tourist.' Mark figured he should enjoy what Los Angeles and the surrounding area had to offer before he was swamped with work and years passed before he ever set foot on the Walk of Stars or in the Chinese Theatre. "I don't mind doing things on my own," he told Anna, "but I'd love if you'd be my tour guide today. If you have time?"

How could Anna say no? He was an old acquaintance, a dear friend of her brother, really. And she was the only person he knew in the area. "I'd be happy to," she answered and was rewarded with his disarming smile.

THREE

Anna almost tripped over Nick's luggage in the foyer when she entered the house. She heard movement and proceeded up the staircase following sounds to the master bedroom. She stopped at the entrance to the room and leaned against the doorjamb. Anna watched Nick remove his shirt over his head, his tight abs flexing as he moved. He leaned one hand against the wall for balance while he took off his socks. Then he slid his jeans to the floor. Barefoot, shirtless, and standing in his boxer briefs, he was quite a tantalizing sight. He pushed his jet-black hair out of his emerald green eyes. It was getting too long and needed to be cut. She loved the way his hair at the nape of his neck and sideburns started to curl as it got too long for his liking. He turned fully towards the doorway and met Anna's eyes.

Smiling, he said, "I didn't hear you come home. I thought I'd take a shower. After all that traveling, I feel gross. Did you get some lunch?"

"Yes, actually. I met up with an old acquaintance. I

don't know if I ever mentioned an old college friend of Josh's. He moved to the area last week and took me to lunch today." She paused to see if Nick showed any interest.

"What's his name? Maybe I'd recognize it." Nick asked as he entered the master bathroom and turned on the overhead rain shower.

"Mark Williams," Anna answered over the bombilation of raindrops.

"No, can't say it sounds familiar. I'll be out in a minute," Nick called back to Anna as the water spray soaked his hair.

Nick hoped Anna wasn't too upset about the delay. He knew they hadn't been connecting and wanted to make it up to her. And who wouldn't want to? His wife was absolutely perfect; smart, sweet, and sexy. He didn't even mind her occasional bouts of stage fright. Her inability to be in the spotlight was rarely an issue in their day-to-day lives. He usually wouldn't think twice about it, but found it ironic as his entire career rests on people wanting the limelight. Anna is the exact opposite of that. She loves to be the cheerleader, encouraging others, but keeps a low profile. He first learned of her stage fright while they were dating. They had gone to a club to see a comedic hypnotist and she almost vomited when the comic tried to get her on stage. Nick didn't care if she went on stage or not. He worried that she was miserable from it, but soon found that it was actually quite rare she found herself in such situations. And he was thankful she was anything but timid when they were alone. No stage fright in the bedroom. He was turned on just thinking about her. He lathered himself from head to toe and let the water rinse the suds down his body.

As Anna waited for Nick, she undressed. She laid her clothes on a chair and crossed the room to the bed. Wearing only her bra and panties, she lay down on the bed, propping herself on her elbow as she flipped through another travel magazine. Not many heterosexual men would pass up a half-naked woman. She heard a buzz and looked at her phone on the side table. It wasn't hers. She rolled over to Nick's side and saw his phone was lit up. All she could read was a name, Cindy D., and part of the message. *"Nick, call me when...."* The rest was cut off, and Anna wasn't going to snoop. It was probably work-related. What Anna would do is turn the phone silent, so there were no further interruptions. She flicked the phone's switch to silent mode and rolled back to her side of the bed.

A few moments later, Nick came out of the bathroom with an oversized-towel wrapped around his waist. Anna assumed he would head into the walk-in closet to get dressed, but she was pleasantly surprised when he headed directly toward her and told her to kneel on the bed.

Nick placed his hands on her waist and drew her to him. "Hi. I missed you," he said in his deep voice, planting kisses along her jawline, down her neck and along her clavicle. His breath warming her sensitive skin at each kiss.

"I missed you, too," Anna replied, reciprocating with gentle kisses on his neck and shoulders, searing his skin where her lips touched. Making their way up, their lips connected. At first, the kiss was soft and sweet, but soon turned hungry and greedy. After three weeks apart, they weren't able to get enough of each other. Anna fisted her hand in Nick's hair as he spread his palms across her back. He felt her bra straps and followed the fabric to her shoulders, pushing the straps down her upper arms. Sliding both hands forward, he moved the white lace mesh below her breast and stroked each nipple with his thumbs. His relentless ministrations were overwhelming, her underwear damp in anticipation. Nick dipped his head lower and took one taut nipple into his mouth. Nipping, sucking, teasing her until she bucked forward, trying to find him so she could grind herself against him. Nick's hands skimmed down her body, steadying her hips. He wrapped one hand around her, grabbing her butt while his other hand snuck between her legs sliding along her dampened underwear. He eased the material aside and let his fingers glide along her slick vulva.

"I want you. Now," Anna demanded.

"Ditto, babe," he told her as he slid her underwear down her thighs and helped her out of them. Nick gently laid Anna back against the pillows and eased her legs open as he ripped the towel from his waist and tossed it aside. Anna saw he was as ready as she was. Nick reached into the drawer of the side table, found a condom, tore it open, and slid it down his erect length.

Anna held her breath at the site of him, ready to take him in. He poised himself over her delaying the moment they'd both been waiting for. He slid inch by inch into her as she pushed her hips up to meet him. Nick couldn't remember the last time he was inside Anna, but he knew he wouldn't forget this. She felt warm and soft and fit so well. He put his fingers between them, just above where they joined, rubbing up and down as he slowly pulled out and pushed back inside. He felt her tighten around him as she got closer, and had to steady himself while he continued to sweep his fingers along her sensitive nub. She gently guided his hand away, and their bodies moved together, a delicious pressure building inside. Nick nipped at her shoulder as he continued to slam into her. Anna's nails raked his back, holding on until her insides melted as they climaxed together.

Anna's body felt languid after being so thoroughly loved. She missed this. This closeness. Everything felt right again when they were together. Any doubts vanished from her mind as she felt the weight of Nick on top of her. He leaned on one elbow and looked intensely into the depths of her dark eyes, then kissed her neck and rolled off of her.

***

After dozing, Anna woke with a smile on her face. She stretched her arms out, hoping to reach Nick, instead touched the pillow on his empty side. The bedroom door was slightly ajar, and she could hear Nick's voice. She couldn't make out what he was saying, but his speech pattern indicated a one-sided conversation. He was on the phone. Anna got out of bed and pushed the door closed the rest of the way. Heading into the bathroom, she realized she was frowning as she turned on the shower. No doubt, he was returning that phone call from earlier. What was that name again? It started with a C...Cindy. Anna didn't recognize the name, as she generally knew the members of Nick's production team. The long work hours created a pretty tight-knit group. She'd have to ask Nick about her. A knock on the bathroom door interrupted her thoughts.

"Hey, hon. I've got some phone calls to make and some work to do before dinner. How do you feel about dinner at La Scala's at eight?" Nick asked through the closed door.

Anna smiled at the fact he wanted to take her out. "That sounds perfect! If you are busy for a while, I'm going to see if I can catch up with Lauren and Beth."

"Sounds like a plan," Nick said, cracking the door open and peeking at his wife.

As Anna started into the shower, she remembered to ask, "Nick, I happened to see you had a missed call from someone named Cindy. Who's that?"

Nick looked Anna in the eyes as he entered the bathroom and replied, "Cynthia is my new assistant producer. She's been on board for almost a month. I thought I mentioned her to you, no?" With their crazy schedules, maybe he hadn't mentioned it. Cynthia was a last-minute hire when his previous assistant producer left them high and dry to work for a competitor.

"Maybe. Just wanted to know about any strange women calling you," Anna teased, placing one hand under the water to test the temperature.

"I'm going to head out, shall I meet you at dinner then?" Nick asked as he brushed his hair in the mirror.

Anna was a little surprised he didn't want to drive together. "I thought we'd meet back here and go to dinner together."

"I don't want to pull you away from your girls and have you waiting around. I want to get as much done as possible today, so I can relax with you tomorrow. It just makes sense to meet at the restaurant." Technically it did make sense because the restaurant was halfway between his office and their home.

Still unsure, Anna said, "If that's what you want."

He turned away from the mirror, leaving his brush on the counter, and grabbed Anna around the waist, pulling her close. His clothing felt rough against her smooth, naked skin. "What I want is to have dinner with you tonight and be able to lounge in bed all day tomorrow with you." He gave her a chaste kiss and released her. "Have fun with Beth and Lauren." He jogged out of the room with a smile on his face, grabbing his keys, bag, and laptop. Nick was looking forward to tonight.

Anna finished her shower and stood in her closet, staring at a wall of clothes. This feels too familiar, she thought. Getting ready for a date night with Nick, with an unsettling feeling in her stomach. Would he actually be at dinner tonight? As she perused her choices of dress, she remembered she needed to confirm with Bethany. She sent a quick text saying she was free for a few hours, and the house was empty with Nick running out to work. A few minutes later, Bethany confirmed she'd be over. Bethany also relayed the message that Lauren was up for some girl time, too. Anna took her time putting on a deep purple wrap dress and picked out a pair of black boots. Anna enjoyed the cool May evenings in California and the refreshing air that reminded her of early autumn on the east coast.

Anna set out three water glasses, iced tea, and some cheese and crackers. When the doorbell rang, she hopped up from the kitchen counter stool and practically skipped to the door. She threw open the door and bear-hugged her girlfriends. Bethany and Lauren squeaked hello as they waited for Anna to release them. Anna's two closest friends were a study of contrasts. Where Bethany was blonde and curvy, Lauren was auburn-haired, tall, and slender. Bethany's crystal blue eyes showcased every emotion she felt, while Lauren's deep sea-green eyes held her secrets. Anna loved these girls and how they looked like Charlie's Angels when they all went out together.

"You're finally here! I've been dying to have time with you two." Anna ushered them inside. "Is iced tea okay, or did either of you want something a little stronger?" Lauren and Bethany placed their bags on the counter as they entered the kitchen.

"Iced tea is fine with me." Bethany started pouring herself a glass.

Lauren eyed Anna and pulled a bottle of wine out of her tote bag. "I brought something a little stronger. Beth's my driver tonight. Am I pouring for two, Anna?"

Anna contemplated her options. "I'll stick to iced tea for now, I'm driving to dinner later. Let me get you a glass for that." Anna reached into the cupboard as Lauren pretended to drink the bottle. "Opener is over there." Anna pointed across the kitchen. "I take it you're feeling better."

"Yes, much. Thank you," Lauren took the wine glass from Anna. After the drinks were poured, they carried their beverages and the cheese plate into the adjoining sitting area. Anna placed the platter on the glass cocktail table and sat in an oversized armchair while Lauren and Bethany sat across on the L-shaped sofa. The last hours of sunlight lit the room through the floor to ceiling windows.

"So, how are things going with Drew?" Anna asked Bethany. Bethany owned a clothing boutique where she met Drew, one of her suppliers. For months Bethany has coyly mentioned her interest in Drew to Anna and Lauren.

Bethany tucked one leg under her and nestled into the sofa cushion. "Well, let's just say we are having a nice time. I'm not sure what to make of our relationship," Bethany said, using her fingers to make air quotes. "He seemed really interested and asked me out, finally, after weeks of flirting." Sipping her drink she continued, "So last night, Drew *escorted* me to an art opening of one of his friends, Justin Turnbull. Apparently, Justin is an up and coming artist. You know that little gallery we pass opposite the pier when you're heading toward Très Chic?" Bethany was referring to her clothing store located in the downtown area of Santa Monica. "Well, that is where we were last night. Very cozy gallery, not one of those pretentious exhibits with lots of blank walls. His paintings are so beautiful and sensuous. Anyway, it was an amazing event. The food was outstanding, the drinks were flowing, I had a great time, and I thought he did, too. But then, when he dropped me off at the end of the night, nothing happened. Nada. Zip. He practically bolted when I asked if he wanted to come up to my apartment when he brought me home." She huffed out a breath, "It was so awkward. I'm not going to call him. After that, he needs to call me if he wants to see me again. I felt terrible after he left me last night. I don't get it. Have I been relegated to *friend*?"

Lauren took a sip of her wine and said, "Beth, I think you are taking it too personally." Lauren turned to Anna to explain. "When I was in Beth's shop last Sunday, you should have heard them. I tried not to stare, but the way he was looking at her, I thought he was going to have her for lunch." Turning back to Bethany, she added, "From the flirting I heard between you two, he is definitely into you. If he were going to use you, he would have taken you up on your offer, don't you think? There must be some other reason he left so quickly."

"I don't know, and right now, I don't want to think about it." Looking to change the subject, Bethany asked, "Anna, what's going on with you and Nick? Last time we talked, you were saying how you two were barely home at the same time."

Anna slowly sipped her tea, thinking about how much she should share with her two closest friends. She felt like she was over-analyzing everything. She and Nick were both very busy people, but when they were together, it was phantasmagoric. "I guess I've been feeling neglected. Nick has been so busy with work. I knew when I met him how crazy his life was, but I feel like somehow he made more time for me back then, when we were dating, and even in the early part of our marriage. Now that we're past the honey-moon stage, it seems that it's easy for him to put me second," she paused, then added, "if not last." She looked at her friends and couldn't quite decipher the looks on their faces. Was it pity? "I can't believe I'm complaining about this. I have a wonderful husband who works extremely hard. I shouldn't complain. He's taking me out for a romantic dinner tonight. I think I've just been missing him. And it didn't help running into an old crush last night." Anna hadn't meant for that to slip out.

Beth perked up. "Who is this you're talking about?"

"Do tell," Lauren added, placing her wine glass on the coffee table and sitting forward, giving Anna her full attention.

Anna went on to tell them how she ran into Mark and knew him through her brother, Josh. "Wait, you didn't just run into him, but saw him today? This morning?" Lauren questioned Anna.

Anna timidly replied, "Yes, this morning into the afternoon. We met for coffee and then went for a tour of Hollywood Boulevard. Did a few touristy things since he's new to the area."

Beth asked, "But what does seeing Mark have to do with you and Nick?"

"I get it," Lauren interrupted, "You're feeling neglected by Nick, and then WHAM a cutie from the past appears, drooling for you."

"I wouldn't say drooling," Anna said defensively, "Mark was just looking for a friendly face to help him settle in town. I probably won't even hear from him again. He starts work at his new law firm next week and will be buried in briefs."

"I'm sure," Lauren wiggled her eyebrows and quipped, "whose briefs is the question?" All three women burst into laughter.

FOUR

At seven-fifteen, Bethany grabbed her car keys and ushered a tipsy Lauren out of Anna's house. Anna hugged each friend goodbye and grabbed her purse to freshen up before heading out to meet Nick for dinner.

Anna arrived at La Scala in Beverly Hills ten minutes before eight. She left her car with the valet and headed toward the restaurant door. As Anna walked across the sidewalk, she felt calm, happiness settling in her chest. She looked up at La Scala's awning, where hundreds of twinkle lights dangled and glowed, giving an ethereal feel to the restaurant entrance. Entering the restaurant, she inhaled the delightful scent of garlic and warm Italian bread. She smiled and gave her name to the attractive hostess who greeted her. Not surprisingly, Nick had reserved a round booth, which was much too large for just the two of them. She slid onto the empty bench and asked for a gin and tonic after being greeted by a waiter who introduced himself as Marco. Water glasses were filled, and Marco produced her drink with a flourish. Anna took a sip and glanced at her watch. Seven minutes past eight.

Just as her happiness began to wane, she saw Nick enter the restaurant. Relief flooded Anna, and a huge smile filled her face as Nick spoke to the hostess and gestured toward Anna at the table. Anna started salivating like Pavlov's dog at the sight of her husband. Anna's focus was entirely on Nick. His dark hair was pushed back with a few curls starting to fall forward. He wore a dark suit with no tie, and his white shirt was left unbuttoned at the top.

Suddenly, Anna's vision was filled with a woman's figure clad in black. Anna looked from the svelte figure up to a long, smooth neck, pouty rose-colored lips, and large blue eyes hooded with the longest lashes Anna had ever seen. The woman's face was framed by flowing golden waves of hair that hung just above her well-endowed chest. This woman was gorgeous. Anna's heart sank as she realized the woman was being ushered to the table by Nick.

"Babe, this is Cynthia Diaz, my assistant producer." Anna pasted a smile on her face as she said hello, keeping her hands in her lap under the table. At Anna's questioning look, Nick went on to explain, "Cindy was on her own tonight, and I really wanted you two to meet. My work wife and my... other...wife... heh heh..." Nick realized his attempt at humor didn't produce a smile from Anna, though Cynthia let out a polite chuckle and excused herself to the ladies' room.

"What's going on, Nick? I thought we were going to have some alone time. Weren't you just working with Cynthia for the last four hours?" Anna let out a deep breath.

Nick could practically see the smoke coming out of Anna's head. Boy had he messed up. "I'm so sorry, babe. We got to talking about you, and when she didn't have plans tonight, I thought it might be fun....", Nick ran a hand through his hair, a nervous habit. "Never mind. I'm sorry. What do you want me to do? *Un*-invite her?"

Anna just stared at Nick and then, in a defeated manner, answered, "Of course not. That would be rude, kind of like inviting someone to join a romantic dinner." She let that sit for a beat then asked, "What exactly did you think would be fun?" Anna probably didn't want to know the answer. Did he think the three of them would hit it off and end up in bed? It would be a little out of character for Nick to want a threesome. That certainly had never come up in their years together. Is she alone not enough anymore?

Before Nick could answer, Marco came over to take his drink order. Nick ordered an Oban neat. A stiff drink for what was shaping up to be an awkward night. After exchanging pleasantries with Marco, Nick looked back at Anna, forgetting what she had asked him. He had to figure out a way to smooth things over and get through dinner as quickly as possible. Maybe Nick would feign illness and take Anna home. He didn't want to upset Cindy, but she would understand his wife's well-being was his priority.

Anna remained quiet, thankful Nick didn't answer

her question. She sipped her drink and watched the doorway leading to the bathrooms, trying to figure out why Nick would intentionally disrupt what was supposed to be a romantic night for the two of them. Anna started to feel a tightening in her chest. This evening, she had been looking forward to, was not going as planned. Her stomach started to feel queasy.

Just as she was about to tell Nick she wasn't feeling well and was going to go home, Cynthia returned to the table. Nick scooted in to make room next to him, but she remained standing. "It was incredibly thoughtful of you, Nick, to invite me to join you and Anna. I just got a phone call, and I will have to take a rain check, if that's all right with you both?" Cynthia looked from Nick to Anna with genuine concern in her eyes.

Anna and Nick couldn't believe their luck. Whether Cynthia felt the tension and was bagging out to avoid an unpleasant time, or she really had received a phone call, neither Anna nor Nick cared. The feigned concern in their eyes belied their true ecstatic feelings. "Is everything okay?" Anna asked.

Cynthia smiled, "Oh, yes. No emergency. I'll leave you two to your evening."

"We'll catch up Monday then," Nick said. He stood and escorted Cynthia to the restaurant entrance.

Anna watched them curiously, still trying to process what Nick was thinking. For some reason, Nick's beautiful assistant producer made Anna feel insecure. Typically, she wouldn't give another beautiful woman a second thought. Anna was comfortable with her looks. But knowing how much time Nick and Cynthia have been spending together, made Anna question whether there might be something more between them. And why were they talking about Anna at work? She watched as Nick hugged Cynthia goodbye and headed back to their table.

"Again, I am so sorry. I don't know what I was thinking," Nick said as he slid back into the booth. Leaning towards Anna, he put his mouth close to her ear and whispered, "Will you forgive me for not thinking clearly?"

His warm breath tickled her ear, and she shrugged her shoulder. "We'll see," is all she said.

"Well, I will start making it up to you instantly," Nick gave an open mouth kiss to her neck, touching his tongue to her sensitive skin, sending a shiver down Anna's spine. It was hard to stay mad when he gave her all of his attention.

Marco cleared his throat, placing Nick's scotch in front of him. "Sorry to disturb you. Would you like to hear tonight's specials?" Anna and Nick nodded for Marco to continue. After he described the dishes he asked, "Would you like to start with an appetizer?"

Nick put his napkin on his lap and motioned for Anna to speak while he composed himself. Asking Nick if he'd share a salad, Anna ordered a half chopped salad and Linguine alle Vongole. Passing the menus to Marco, Nick ordered the Spaghetti alla Bolognese.

Marco headed towards the kitchen and Nick asked Anna about her work and her girlfriends. Anna told Nick about the ending to Beth's date last night.

"He probably got the runs," Nick stated matter-of-factly.

Anna's face contorted at his heinous suggestion. "Ew! Why would you say that? There are a million reasons Drew didn't go up to her apartment. Maybe he didn't want to move the relationship too quickly. Maybe he respects her," Anna offered.

"If what Lauren said is true, that they flirt like crazy, and he looked like he was going to pounce on her in the middle of her store, then the only logical reason a heterosexual man would not go upstairs to continue the evening is because he has to drop a deuce." Nick casually sat back and sipped his drink like they were talking about the weather.

"Oh, my God! I have to tell Beth this! She was so upset that he dropped her off so abruptly after what she thought was a nice time for both of them. She's going to die when she hears your theory: he's either gay or he had diarrhea." They both laughed, imagining telling Beth her options.

Their conversation flowed easily. Anna and Nick got lost in each other's humor and put the incident of Cynthia out of their minds. After the plates were cleared, they decided to forego dessert at the restaurant in favor of dessert at home. At the entrance to the restaurant, Nick handed his and Anna's valet tickets to two young men for their cars to be retrieved. While they waited on the sidewalk, Nick placed his hand in Anna's hair and pulled her against him for a long kiss, promising what was to come. He eased her head away as he heard a car approaching and saw it was Anna's car. Nick walked her to her driver's door, handing the valet a tip. His Q5 pulled up behind her TT as he tucked her inside the vehicle.

"See you at home. Drive carefully," he said, taking in her flushed cheeks and shining eyes. Anna found her voice, "You, too," and slowly closed her car door. She watched Nick in her side mirror walk to his car and climb in, then she fastened her seatbelt and adjusted the rearview. Turning on the radio, she pulled away from the curb. The 30-minute drive home couldn't go by fast enough for Anna. When Nick passed her, honking his horn, she saw he was in a hurry as well.

FIVE

Sunday morning came too soon, almost as quickly as Anna and Nick did the night before. As Anna made her way down the stairs, she picked up the trail of clothes she and Nick had created in their eagerness last night. She smiled as she remembered how frantic they had been to touch and taste each other. They had finally fallen asleep in each other's arms sometime after midnight. Anna carried the clothes into the laundry room, dropping them into the washing machine. She headed into the kitchen to brew a cup of coffee then examined the refrigerator's contents for breakfast food. Planning to make an omelet, she grabbed the egg carton, mushrooms, and some leftover ham. As she turned with the fixings stacked on top of the egg carton, she banged into a solid wall of muscle, causing her breakfast plans to crash to the ground.

"Oops," Nick looked at the mess on the kitchen floor and started picking up the still wrapped mushrooms and ham. "I didn't know I had such an effect on you that you're all butter fingers when I'm in the room," he joked.

Anna grabbed a bunch of paper towels to start mopping up the mess of broken eggs. "Nick! I had no idea you were there—announce yourself next time!" She tried to hide her smile while she scooped up yolk, albumen, and shell. "I was just about to make omelets." She picked up two unbroken eggs. "These two survived. I guess I can make a couple of hard-boiled eggs." Anna rinsed off the unscathed eggs and placed them in a pot. She disinfected the floor while Nick took the eggs from the pan and put them back in the refrigerator. Anna threw out the paper towels and put the disinfectant away. She was about to fill the pot with water when she noticed the eggs were gone. "Hey, where'd they go?"

Nick took Anna by the hand and started to lead her out of the kitchen. "Why don't we go out for breakfast? Come on, we'll get dressed and head to the diner. It's still early enough we should be able to get a table without a long wait."

As they climbed the stairs, Anna looked up at Nick. "I think there's a yoga class at eleven. Do you mind if I run to the gym after breakfast?" The gym where they were both members wasn't far from the diner. Anna changed into yoga pants and a tank top, throwing a long, comfy sweatshirt over it. She went into the bathroom to wash her face, and when she came out, she saw Nick was in a pair of athletic pants and a t-shirt.

"I think going to the gym is a great idea. I'll get in a

workout while you're in yoga class." Nick pumped his arms as if he were curling weights.

"Sounds good to me. Now let's go, I'm starving." Anna grabbed her gym bag as Nick grabbed his, and they headed out.

After yoga, Anna showered and changed into street clothes. She headed to the front of the gym to wait for Nick while he finished in the locker room. As Anna sat in a chair next to the floor to ceiling windows looking out into the parking lot, she spotted a friendly face walking toward the doors. She had forgotten that Nick's co-producer was also a member. As he approached the desk to check-in, Anna called out to him, "Hello, Steven."

Turning at the sound of his name, Steven's face lit up with a genuine smile upon seeing Anna. "It's so nice to see you. It's been forever." Steven walked to Anna, embracing her and kissing her cheek.

"Well, you've been tied up with Nick all over the world. How's Darron?" Anna asked, referring to Steven's husband. "We barely get to see our husbands. You'll have to come over for dinner sometime.

"He's none too pleased with this crazy schedule Nick and I have been running. We are trying to get picked up by a major network and want to do a cable series, so now we're working on a new reality show where couples find their true love. What a hoot! I tell ya, scouting locations for this has been a doozy. Anyway, I told Darron I'd make it up to him, so I just booked a little trip for us to Hawaii." Steven put his index finger to his lips. "Shhh. I haven't told him yet.

We'll take off for a week right after the new show wraps. Obviously, we'll have to have all the pieces in place before we can take a breather, but it looks like we're on schedule."

"My lips are sealed," Anna mimed zipping her lips. She spotted Nick walking down the corridor towards them. "Here comes Nick now."

"I see Nick more than I see Darron," Steven lamented, "The last time I saw Nick at the gym was a couple of weeks ago with his new assistant. Have you met Cynthia? She's absolutely fantastic! You will love her. She's a hard worker, able to keep up with Nick. Those two have been burning the midnight oil. I end up leaving the two of them to get some shut-eye and find out they're usually banging heads together until two in the morning." Just then, Nick joined them. Steven turned to him and said, "Hey Nick, I'm sure you want to get home. I'll catch you tomorrow. What time are you heading to the office in the morning?"

As Nick and Steven worked out their schedule for the following day, Anna's mind started working overtime, analyzing Steven's words. Banging heads together into the middle of the night? Exactly which head was Nick banging with Cynthia? And when was Nick at the gym with her? Nick and Anna talked at least once a day, so she was a little surprised he wouldn't have mentioned it. They always gave each other silly updates on their day. Was he hiding something? Was she overreacting? Steven didn't think anything to say it to Anna. She's known Steven for seven years, as long as she's known Nick. She trusts Steven's judgment. But could Nick be keeping something from Steven as well as her? If Nick hadn't shown up just now, Anna would have asked Steven if he was actually delayed Friday night and flew home Saturday as Nick had. Now Anna was becoming concerned. Her chest squeezed, heart thudding under her breast bone. It was one thing to worry they needed time together to reconnect as a couple. It was another to wonder if he was having an affair.

The thought of an affair brought her sophomore year of college to the forefront of her mind. She remembered being desperately in love with an upperclassman named Matteo. Matteo was the life of the party, charismatic, and easy on the eyes, with golden hair and irides the color of the Caribbean Sea. She also remembered feeling as if she'd won the lottery having his affection returned. He had courted her from the moment she had walked into sociology class and sat in the empty seat beside him.

Matteo was in his fourth year but had to fulfill a basic graduation requirement, landing him in a mid-level sociology class. The class was small, only fifteen students, so it was easy to develop a rapport with all of the classmates. And it seemed Matteo gave most of his attention to Anna. She got lost in the crystal depths of his eyes as he stared intently at her every morning as she entered the class. He always made a point of saving the seat next to him and initiating conversation. After a few weeks of flirting he asked her out. A few more weeks of spending her weekends with him, and they were exclusive.

The first semester whirled by with laughter and teasing, meeting up to walk to the shared class together, bumping into each other at the library or meeting for meals at the campus eatery. They spent so much time together that people they didn't even know recognized them as a couple.

When winter break rolled around, Anna took a flight back to Connecticut and Matteo to his hometown in Santa Rosa, New Mexico. They would text or talk almost daily, until he surprised her between Christmas and New Year's. He had taken the initiative to contact her parents for permission to visit for three days before joining his parents for skiing in Stowe, Vermont. Anna remembered his family would trade time at various ski resorts every winter. Sometimes in Vail, Colorado, Vermont, Maine, sometimes Whistler or Mont Tremblant in Canada. Always changing, so it was a happy coincidence they had planned for New England this particular year. When they returned to campus for the second semester, Anna couldn't imagine a happier time. Matteo's thoughtfulness and attentiveness had her heart falling for this man she knew would be graduating in a few months time. Matteo brought up the idea of them spending spring break together with a small group of friends in Miami, so that is what they did.

Shortly after spring break, Matteo received his acceptance letter to Tulane Medical School, his first choice. They celebrated with friends that weekend and Matteo talked of how they would continue to see each other the following year, telling Anna she was the world to him.

With only a few weeks left to the semester, Matteo's behavior began to change. Anna had been young and naïve and hadn't paid attention fully to the signs that everything wasn't as it had been. They were little things, but added up in hindsight, it was clear he wasn't faithful, and Anna had gullibly believed all the excuses he had told her. She attributed this change to the stress of final exams, the forthcoming summer break and their imminent separation.

First it was his vague responses about where he was or who he was with, claiming she was being clingy. She didn't think she was insecure - she didn't need to know where he was every second of every day but if she was going to be with girlfriends on a Friday evening, she told him so, even where they would be going.

He didn't like surprise visits either. He told her to text him to let him know she was on the way over to his place, under the guise of wanting to meet her, or have the place straightened for her. And it never was particularly clean when she arrived to his suite, shared with five other guys. And then there was the time another young woman came to his room to retrieve a watch she had left the night before. Anna didn't give it much thought as he claimed they had been studying together for an exam. Anna had been very trusting. Too trusting.

The first week of exams Anna didn't text him ahead of time, making an impromptu decision to visit his suite to ask if he wanted to join her for brunch. One of his roommates was leaving as she arrived and let her in, unbeknownst to her and the roommate, that same woman was in Matteo's room. He came out of his room in a pair of boxers, leaving the bedroom door slightly ajar with Anna having a clear view of the woman getting dressed. There wasn't any need for a conversation. Anna left and ignored him until he stopped calling. She wished she could say she didn't shed any tears, but she felt like a fool. Not only to have let herself fall in love, but to imagine a future with him. The experience had toughened her and opened her eyes to the harsh reality that not everyone is trustworthy.

Anna didn't let the affair stop her from dating, but it did have her shielding her heart. Nick was the first one to break through her defenses and even that took a leap of faith.

Anna was pulled back into the conversation when Steven said, "Anna, I'll talk to Darron about dinner. When did you have in mind?"

Anna pursed her lips together as she thought about what she might have scheduled during the week.

"Let's look at Friday night." Anna pulled up the calendar on her phone to confirm she was free. "If you two don't think you'll have to work terribly late, we can plan for seven. Just let me know if that will work." Steven nodded and told Anna he would let Nick know early this week.

As Steven walked away, Anna turned to Nick. "I assume Friday will work for you?"

Nick pulled Anna close and whispered into her ear,

"Perhaps I was planning to have a hot date that night." Anna could smell his body wash and felt his warm breath. She started to lean into him as she registered what he had said. "What do you mean? With who exactly?" Anna couldn't believe he would actually say that to her. Admit he would have a date with someone else. She felt her ire begin to rise, creating tension in her neck and shoulders. Now he was being cavalier with their marriage? When did he start to think they had an open relationship?

Lines of confusion creased Nick's face. He took in Anna's furrowed brow and her arms, now crossed. She looked upset. "I'm pretty sure there's only one woman I would want to have on that hot date. You're teasing me." He sighed in relief. "For a second, you looked genuinely pissed. You're the only one for me, babe." Nick put his arms around Anna and rocked her gently. "Come on, babe, let's get home. You can show me some of your yoga moves." Anna tried to shake off her mood. She tried to believe Nick was, in fact, talking about her as the hot date. Anna had to get herself under control. She couldn't just blow up at him every time she heard he had to work late with this new assistant producer....Cynthia.

She was beginning to hate the name.

She let Nick guide her to his car and open the door for her. He looked at her as she climbed in. He could tell something was wrong. Her mood was sullen and not as carefree as it had been all morning. He didn't know what happened while they were apart at the gym, but something must have happened for her mood to change so drastically. She wasn't usually a particularly moody person.

"Anna, did something happen while we were at the gym? You seem upset." Nick wasn't sure if he'd get a straight answer out of her, but he had to try. He wanted more than anything to see her face light up again.

"I'm really not sure. Steven said in passing you've been spending a lot of time with your new assistant producer. An assistant producer you hadn't mentioned to me. Now, I find out you're at the gym together, inviting her to our dinner, and working late into the night, alone with her. Nick, is there something you need to tell me?" Anna held her breath, waiting for a response. She honestly didn't know if she wanted to know the answer to her question.

Nick let out a chuckle.

"What?" Anna questioned his laughter.

"Honestly? I'm flattered. Who knew my wife could get rattled so easily? Are you jealous of me spending time with my colleagues?" Nick took her hand. "You have nothing to worry about. I'd think you'd know that. When the projects are progressing, you know I practically live with Steven and my team."

"I do know that. I actually have been thinking a lot about us having some time away together. I was looking at a travel magazine and imaging us somewhere warm, lounging by a pool." Anna felt like she'd been on a rollercoaster. Her emotions went from serenity to agitation and back again in the blink of an eye. I guess this is what it feels like to love someone with every part of your being. It wasn't always this way. Even with Nick's crazy schedule, why was she feeling so insecure now?

Nick responded simply with a "Hmmm, that sounds nice." Then he added almost as an after-thought. "We'll have to look at when we can make that happen." He put his lips to hers and slowly pulled away. "Let's get home so I can finish that thought." Then he winked and put the car into drive.

The rest of Sunday felt decadent. They lounged in the TV room, watching 100 Humans on Netflix, chatted over a glass of wine, and cooked dinner together after having stopped at the store on their way back from the gym. By the time Anna fell asleep in Nick's arms, she was feeling relaxed. If only she could have held on to that feeling come Monday morning.

SIX

Anna generally woke up before Nick when he was working in LA. She liked to be in her office early to answer emails before colleagues knocked on her door for a 'good morning' chat. Anna tended to be out the door by eight o'clock to tackle the 20-minute commute in the traffic typical of the area. The mere six miles to AC Technologies, the computer-consulting firm where she worked, was usually a crawl. She rarely set her alarm, and this morning was no different except Anna woke to an empty bed.

Nick was towel-drying his hair as she entered the bathroom. He wore his slacks but was still bare-chested. She watched water droplets glide down his chest before he put the towel around his shoulders. She gave him a kiss as she passed by. "You're up early," Anna commented. "Usually, I'm already downstairs by the time you get up."

Nick styled his hair as he spoke. "I told Steven I'd try to get in early so we can wrap up, hopefully, a little early today. He wants to make sure he's home for an early dinner and show with Darron, and I thought that's a great idea. We can meet for dinner if you don't have a late day."

"Let me get back to you on that." Anna was thrilled that Nick wanted to try to have an earlier than usual evening, but she knew her workload was going to be pretty heavy this week. "I'll see what I can do, but I can't make any promises to be done before 6:30pm. We're on a tight deadline for this phase of implementation." Anna oversaw the technical team of the consulting firm, so her job was to make sure modifications and infrastructure were ready on schedule for 'Go-Live'.

Nick was quiet for a moment before he said, "Don't worry about it. I can grab dinner on the way home." He left the bathroom to finish getting ready and was out the front door before Anna left the bedroom. Anna liked the idea of Nick picking up dinner. That way, they could relax together and not have to think about what to cook.

Anna's day went as expected, moments of calm interspersed with frantic messages from users looking for a fix to expected and unexpected problems. Around three o'clock, her phone buzzed with a text message. She looked at her phone, expecting it to be another work issue when she saw Mark Williams' name on the display.

Mark: *You busy?*

Anna: *Swamped. How are you?*

Mark: *New job is going well. You busy for dinner to-*

night? I thought I'd thank you for being my tour guide this past weekend.

Anna: *Actually I have dinner plans. I can be available tomorrow night. Would that work?*

Mark: *Yes. I'm still learning where to go. You have any recommendations?*

Anna: *Do you like Thai?*

Mark: *Love it.*

Anna's phone buzzed with another message. She quickly looked and saw it was a work message.

Anna: *Great. I'll send you directions. Gotta go. Work.*

Mark: *Work always gets in the way of life.*

Anna: *TTYL*

Anna answered the work issue, worked on some code she needed to revise for a modification, and then marked her calendar *Dinner with Mark, 7pm, at Apsara.*

At twenty-five past six o'clock, she shut down her computer and headed out of the office, looking forward to some takeout with Nick.

When she arrived home, solar-powered lights illuminated the driveway, and the front door's lanterns glowed. Anna was surprised not to see any lights on inside the house. She entered the side entry off the kitchen and found the house dark. Anna flipped on light switches as she put down her purse and keys. Thinking Nick might be relaxing in the den, she walked through the kitchen, noticing nothing seemed disturbed. No food on the counter. No glasses set for drinks. Anna approached the door to the den and called into the dark for Nick. No answer. Heading back into the kitchen, Anna called his cell phone.

She placed her phone on the counter and tapped the screen to turn on the speaker. As Anna listened to his number ringing, she found a wine glass, and filled it from a previously opened bottle. As she poured the burgundy liquid, she heard Nick speak.

"Hey, babe. You home already?"

"Yeah. Where are you?"

"At dinner."

"Oh." Anna was almost speechless. She clearly remembered Nick saying he would grab dinner on his way home. "I thought you were picking up takeout for us."

"Babe, I told you this morning I was going to stop on my way home, so you didn't have to worry about getting home any particular time. Were you waiting for me?" Anna could hear the disquiet in his voice.

"I thought you meant you were going to grab dinner on your way home for us." Anna felt let down, but she knew it was merely a misunderstanding.

"I'm finishing up here. Let me get the check, and I'll be home in half an hour. Want me to order you anything?"

"No, just get home. I can find something here to eat." Anna could now hear a woman's voice in the background. Nick directed his next statement to the woman. "It's Anna. I've got to head home." Then speaking back into the phone, "I'll see you soon."

"Ok. See you soon." Anna pressed the screen to hang up. She solemnly walked to the refrigerator and opened the door looking inside for something quick to throw together. She saw the leftover Chicken Parmesan from Sunday night and heated it in the microwave. As the dinner warmed, Anna took a gulp of wine, poured herself some water, and threw together a salad with some cut up vegetables and lettuce. She made a dressing with olive oil, red wine vinegar, and lemon juice and thought about how quickly things can change. Anna thought the plan was to meet up with Nick; meanwhile, he planned to have dinner with someone else. Anna would bet a million dollars she knew who that someone else was. Cynthia Diaz.

When Nick walked into the kitchen, Anna was sitting in her favorite chair with her feet tucked under her, reading the ipad in her hand. She looked up at Nick and devastated him. Her eyes glistened as if she'd been crying. Nick crossed the kitchen, his long legs carrying him into the seating area with just a few strides. Dropping in front of Anna, he kneeled on the plush carpet in his black trousers, his plum-colored shirt unbuttoned at the neck. Nick gently took the ipad from her hands and placed it on the glass-topped side table. "Babe, I'm so sorry." He held her face in his hands. "I would never intentionally make you cry. I hate to see you hurting, babe."

Anna sniffed and let out a laugh. "I'm not crying over you. It's this book." Nick dropped his hands as Anna gestured towards the device she'd been reading. "I'm not thrilled how we missed each other. I was looking forward to seeing you after work, but it's still early. We can still have a night together." She crossed her arms and raised her eyebrows at him. "You must really think I'm fragile if you think something like this would bring me to tears."

"I didn't know what to think. When I saw tears in your eyes, I just wanted to make it go away." Nick stood up and took both of Anna's hands, tugging her to standing. At 5'11, Nick stood just 4 inches taller than Anna. Her eyes matched up to his mouth. She stared at his lips briefly before she moved her gaze up to his green eyes, which looked closer to blue tonight. She bit her lower lip just before he brought his mouth down to hers. He pressed his lips against hers, waiting for an opening. When her lips remained closed, he pulled back. "But something's wrong," he stated matter-of-factly.

"Who were you with at dinner?" Anna hoped she didn't already know the answer.

"Cynthia." Nick looked at Anna with a blank stare. "Why?"

"It seems you've been spending a lot of time with her."

"You know I spend a lot of time with Steven and Cindy, or whoever my assistant producer is, when we're pushing a new show. What's going on, Anna? This doesn't seem like you to question my work relationships."

Anna felt out of sorts. She realized she must sound like a jealous wife. What was she getting so worked up about? Of course, Nick would have dinner with a work colleague if he didn't think he was going to meet up with her. How can she get upset with Nick when she has dinner plans with Mark tomorrow night?

"Nick, I don't know. For some reason, the fact that

your assistant is a woman is messing with my mind. Let's forget it. I don't want to ruin our night."

Nick put his arms around Anna's waist, and she rested her head on his shoulder. He kissed the top of her head. "Do you want to cuddle up and watch something to distract us?"

"That sounds like a good idea."

Nick eyed the glass of wine on the side table. "Any more of that? I think I could use a drink."

Anna reached for her wine glass and turned towards the kitchen. "Follow me. I've got just what you need."

"I think you've got just what I need, and I'm not talking about the wine." Nick followed her into the kitchen, watching her hips sway as she sashayed to the refrigerator, opening the door and placing the wine bottle onto the island. She took a glass down from the cupboard. "Help yourself," Anna said, giving Nick a devilish smile. "I think I will," Nick retorted. He poured some wine into the glass, sealed the bottle, and took Anna by the hand. Picking up his own drink, he led Anna out of the kitchen.

SEVEN

On Tuesday morning, Anna's phone dinged with a Calendar reminder, as she placed her mug into the kitchen sink.

Dinner with Mark, 7pm, Apsara.

Anna cursed under her breath. "I forgot to send Mark the address." She hastily texted the restaurant name and location. *See you at 7pm?* She typed out.

Mark's text dinged in response. *Looking forward to it.*

"What are you smiling about?" Nick's voice made Anna jump as he entered the kitchen.

"I was just confirming dinner with that friend I told you about." Anna smiled at Nick and tucked her phone into the side pocket of her purse.

"Oh, right. Is this that Mark fellow?" Nick eyed Anna sideways as he asked. He poured himself a glass of orange juice and added: "I thought you had done your good deed this past weekend, showing him around town."

Anna thought she heard a hint of jealousy in Nick's

statement. Good, maybe he'll see how it feels to be second fiddle, she thought. As Nick gulped down the juice, she replied, "Yes, it is. And I've known him for ages, so when he asked me to dinner, I accepted. What will you be doing for dinner tonight?"

Nick placed the glass in the sink. "I'll probably eat with Steven and Cindy, or come back here and order something." Nick picked up his bag from the table by the kitchen doorway, getting ready to leave. "You ready to head out?" he asked Anna as she put her purse on her shoulder and nodded in response.

They walked out together, Nick locking the house behind them. Nick kissed Anna on the cheek, telling her to have a good day. "You, too," she replied as she pulled her car door closed. *I hope he is jealous* she thought to herself as she started the car and looked over at Nick sitting in his driver's seat. Anna smiled at Nick, giving a quick wave, and pulled the car out of the driveway.

As Anna's workday dragged on, she started to think about Nick and Cindy. And Mark. Why was she going to dinner with him so soon after they spent half of Saturday together? She felt an attraction to Mark and knowing that made meeting him alone all the more dangerous. Anna needed backup. And she knew just the redhead to drag into this fiasco.

Anna picked up her phone, dialing Lauren's number as she whirled her desk chair away from her computer screen. Lauren picked up after five rings. Anna heard Lauren speak to someone else before saying into the phone, "Lauren Simpson." Lauren must not have looked at her phone's caller id.

"Hey, Lauren, you sound busy, I'll make it short. Dinner tonight, seven o'clock at Apsara. You in?"

Lauren blew out a breath of air. "Thank God, it's you, Anna. I think I would have lost it if I had to handle one more call from Mr. Gilchrist. He is the neediest client I've had in a while. And they are ALL needy." Like Anna, Lauren worked at AC Technologies; however, Lauren dealt in financials. When there are tech problems in the finance world, people get particularly upset.

"Dinner, Lauren? You'd be doing me a huge favor." Anna begged.

"How is going to dinner with you doing you a favor.... oh, to keep you busy?" Lauren was always jumping to conclusions, barely able to listen to a full story before jumping in with her own thoughts.

"Actually, it'd be me, you, and...Mark Williams. I need a buffer," Anna admitted.

Lauren flipped through her calendar for the day. "I'm in. See you later, lady." Lauren disconnected the phone before Anna could thank her.

Anna decided she shouldn't spring on Mark that she wasn't meeting him alone. She shot off a quick text and practically held her breath, waiting for a response.

Sounds great. I look forward to seeing you and meeting Lauren. See you tonight!

The rest of Anna's day flew by. Shortly after six-thirty, she packed up her computer and headed out of the building.

When she arrived at Apsara's parking lot, Anna texted Lauren and Mark to let them know she was there. She entered the restaurant and scanned the room. Her phone buzzed with a response from Lauren.

Mark and I are seated in the back room. And OMG! You didn't tell me he's hot!

Anna smiled at her friend's not so subtle observation. Greeting the hostess, Anna gestured towards the back room. "I'm joining my friends." The hostess led Anna to a seating area separated from the main dining room by a beautifully hand-painted screen. The hostess pointed to the only occupied table and left Anna to join her friends.

As Anna entered the smaller space, she saw Lauren and Mark leaning into each other laughing. Lauren's red hair was swept to one side, cascading down her shoulder as she gazed into Mark's eyes. Mark's shoulder pressed against Lauren's as he chuckled. Anna felt a weight lift from her shoulders, and her chest tightened as she realized she was thrilled to see Mark and Lauren getting along so well. And just as Anna was considering to retreat to give these two a dinner date alone, Mark looked up and spotted her. She continued to walk toward the table as Mark pushed out of his chair to meet her. He bent slightly pulling her into an embrace, kissing her lightly on the cheek. Anna chose the seat across from Mark as he said, "This is quite a treat. Getting to dine with two beautiful women tonight."

Lauren supplied, "And getting to pick the brains of two successful IT goddesses." Addressing Anna, Lauren continued, "Mark and I arrived about 15 minutes early, giving us time to realize we were both waiting for you." Turning her head to look at Mark, she added, "And for me to learn that Mark can use word and excel, after that he's hopeless."

Mark raised his eyebrows at Lauren and responded, "I wouldn't say hopeless. Sorry to say not everyone is well-versed in SQL or JAVA."

"Okay. Enough shop talk. I'm starving. Let's figure out what we're ordering." Lauren picked up her menu, scanning it but already knowing she was going to order her favorite Pad Thai with chicken. Lauren peeked at Mark, and when she saw he was concentrating on his dinner choices, she mouthed to Anna, "Thank you." Feeling smug, Anna looked back down at her menu.

Dinner was ordered, and the conversation was easy between the three. Anna didn't miss the way Mark and Lauren found ways to touch one another in some way during the dinner, even sharing food as if they've known each other forever.

As the threesome got ready to say their goodbyes, Mark asked Lauren if he could have her number. After they exchanged numbers, Mark hugged Anna and whispered, "Thank you for meeting me and inviting Lauren. She's great. We'll have to plan another get-together."

"Absolutely," Anna replied, unsure if he meant with her or Lauren or both.

They all made their way to the parking lot, waved a goodbye and opened their car doors. Lauren held up a finger to Anna, indicating for her to wait a moment before getting into her vehicle. The women watched Mark drive away, giving another wave goodbye. Then Lauren walked over to Anna, leaving her Range Rover door ajar.

"Anna, Mark seems really great. He asked if he could call me."

"That's awesome, Lauren."

"Is there anything wrong with him? Anything I should know? Because I can see myself really liking him." The look of consternation on Lauren's face spoke volumes to Anna.

"Mark is a really great guy. He and my brother have been friends forever. He has always been a gentleman. I promise, unless he has some deep dark secret, he is an upstanding guy."

Relief flooded Lauren. "Thank God. I'll be pretty sad if he has some weird inclination for nasolingus or something. I don't want my nose sucked. Blech." Lauren hugged Anna before hustling back to her car and getting in.

She rolled down her window and shouted, "Thank you! I'll call you tomorrow." Then backed out of the parking space and drove out of the parking lot. Anna climbed into her car with a smile on her face. Happy for her friends to have found each other and contented that she was the reason they met.

EIGHT

When Anna got home, she found Nick on the couch with his laptop resting on his thighs. The TV was on low volume with a basketball game playing. Several lamps cast a warm glow throughout the room. As she settled onto the couch, tucking her bare feet under her, Nick closed the laptop and put it aside. Wrapping his arm around Anna, he kissed her on the head. "How was dinner with Mark?"

Anna kept her head nuzzled into Nick's shoulder as she answered. "Great." She planned to make this as difficult as possible for Nick. She still held a grudge about the miscommunication and his lack of mentioning his stunning female coworker, who he spends more time with than her.

Nick didn't seem to care that she didn't expand on her evening. He simply moved on with, "Do you have a particularly busy next week?"

Anna wondered if this meant he wanted to make sure they didn't have any more mishaps. "This is my rough week. Next week should be back to support for a while."

"Good. Can you take next week off?" A slight smile played on Nick's lips as he watched Anna's eyes go wide.

"What!?" Anna sputtered. "This is such short notice. And what exactly will I be doing with my time off?"

"Come with me," Anna waited for Nick to finish, "to Santorini."

Anna couldn't believe her ears. A getaway with Nick was exactly what she had been craving. This was a dream come true!

"Greece!" Anna jumped into Nick's lap, showering him with kisses. "Yes! I will let work know. When do we leave?"

Nick cradled Anna as she straddled his lap. "Saturday, if you think you can be packed and ready to go."

Anna hugged Nick tightly. "I will be ready. Thank you, Nick! This is just what we need!"

Nick pulled Anna back so he could look her in the face. "There is one thing you need to know."

Anna didn't like the severity of Nick's tone. "What is it?"

"I will be working on this trip."

"Oh." Anna held her immediate thoughts as Nick continued.

"The network has ordered our pitch direct to series. We will be filming all 13 episodes in a span of a few weeks. We've picked Santorini as the location." Nick caught the look of dismay on Anna's face. "Don't look so worried. We will have plenty of time to relax and have dinners together. We will only film during the week, so the evenings and weekends will be ours."

Anna took a deep breath and exhaled as she slid off Nick's lap to sit beside him. "It's okay, Nick. Just go. I'll stay here, and we can plan a vacation when you are done. I think Steven and Darron are taking a trip soon. Maybe we can double with them."

Nick turned to face her. "Anna, Greece will be amazing. I need you there. Please come." Taking Anna's hand, Nick stared into Anna's eyes. He lowered his face to hers and gave her his best sad puppy dog look.

Anna was just about to give in when Nick's phone buzzed. They both looked at the screen and saw Cynthia Diaz's name flash across it. "Go ahead and answer."

Nick sighed and flicked his finger across the screen, answering the call. He stood up from the couch and walked out of the room as he spoke into the phone, saying, "Give me a minute."

Anna flopped against the couch cushion and let her head fall backward, deflated. She would have loved to go to Santorini with Nick, but not when he'll be working the majority of the time with Cynthia! Anna imagined Cindy and Nick having evening dinners on a romantic island, taking boat rides, and lounging by the water 'working.' *Ugh,* thought Anna, *Why would I let them be alone on a Mediterranean island when Nick just invited me? I must be crazy not to take him up on this.* Anna became resolute. "I am going to Greece!"

NINE

"What time did Steven say they'd be arriving?" Anna shouted from the kitchen out to Nick on the patio.

As Nick preheated the grill, he called back, "They should be here around seven. He said he had to make a quick stop after picking up Darron."

It was Friday evening, and Anna was excited to have the guys over for a relaxing dinner of grilled steaks and salad before their flight Saturday. Over the last two days, Anna made arrangements at work to be away for the entire next two weeks and spent several hours packing and unpacking various outfits. She found packing for the weather not too tricky, as it was similar temperatures in Santorini as Santa Monica this time of year. Thankfully her passport didn't expire for another five years, and Nick had already made arrangements for exchanging currency.

Anna finished making the dressing for the Greek salad they would eat in anticipation of their travel. Nick had informed Anna of the details for the show schedule. Everyone involved would arrive over the weekend, giving them some time to adjust to the time difference before filming commenced on Monday. Filming would continue over roughly 10 days then back to the states to edit and have the show ready to air in September for the start of a new season, assuming the network didn't scrap the show at any point, which wasn't out of the question. Anna didn't know much about the actual show, only what Steven had told her earlier: People finding their true loves. She guessed a lot of work had gone into the pre-planning because the idea was that the 'true loves' would be on the island together. The long hours of work they had been doing was partly tracking down people who the contestants claimed were loves lost; people in their lives that for one reason or another were separated even though they felt were their true love. Anna was starting to get curious what this would look like and hoped she'd be able to watch some of the taping.

The doorbell chimed, interrupting her thoughts. She put the dressing and salad in the fridge as Nick walked past her towards the front hall. He came back into the kitchen, trailing Steven and Darron.

Darron handed Anna a bottle of Jordan Chardonnay as he hugged her hello. "Do you want me to open this now?" she asked after accepting a hug from Steven.

"Might as well," Nick said as he hugged his friends. "Let's have a pre-dinner glass. The steaks will be ready in a matter of minutes once we throw them on the grill."

As Nick tended the grill, Steven kept him company.

Anna could hear their muffled conversation through the open patio doors. A cool breeze ran through the house and ruffled the wisps of hair on Anna's temple. She brushed the strands out of her face and continued to set plates on the long wooden dining table inside the oversized kitchen. Darron placed utensils beside each dish. Anna brought the salad to the table, and asked Darron to retrieve a bottle of wine from the wine cabinet. Holding up the bottle, he asked, "Shall we open a red to go with the steaks?"

"That sounds good to me. Will you open it, let it breathe?" She motioned toward the shelf behind him for the wine opener and an aerator. Darron stripped the foil wrapper from the bottle tip and placed the wine opener over the corked top. "Are you ready for your trip?" he asked as he pulled the cork from the bottle.

"I think so. Thankfully we have a late morning flight giving me time to double and triple-check that I have everything. I'm looking forward to it. I wasn't sure if I would go when Nick told me it's a work trip. But then I figured, why not? I can enjoy the island while he's working and we can be together in the evenings. It's not quite what I had in mind for a vacation, but at least I'll be with him." *And not leave him alone with Cindy Diaz any longer than necessary*, she thought to herself.

Nick's ears perked up when he overheard Darron ask Anna about the trip. He realized this wasn't her idea of a romantic getaway, but he needed her on this trip. He felt like his future happiness depended on it.

***

Twenty hours and 3 layovers later, Anna and Nick arrived on the small island of Santorini. The cab ride from the local airport wound them through small towns until they arrived at a wooden door flanked by white stone walls running in either direction. A gentleman opened the gate for Anna and Nick, directing them to leave their luggage, and escorted them down a few steps into an open courtyard. In the small yard, there were rattan chairs and a loveseat inviting guests to relax. To their right was an infinity pool lined with chaise lounges and umbrellas.

A man dressed in linen slacks and a knit sweater walked out of a small doorway on their left. "Hallo, Mr. and Mrs. Whittaker! Welcome! It is good to see you. How was your trip? You must be ready to relax after such a long flight." George, the proprietor, enthusiastically greeted them. While shaking hands, George peppered them with questions and information in his thick Greek accent.

As George walked them down another set of steep stairs cut into the side of the cliff, he informed them dinner could be brought to their room, or they could eat in the private dining area at the top of the cliffside hotel. Following a path along the side of the cliff and then back up another set of stone stairs, they stopped on a balcony where George inserted the key to open the door to their suite. Anna leaned on the wall of the veranda, looking out. From every direction, Anna glimpsed the Aegean Sea. Looking down the hillside, Anna could see more steps and pathways carved into the face of the cliff with aquamarine swimming pools dotting the bright white façades. Anna breathed in the salty air as she spotted a mass of land across the water. She pointed it out to Nick, who explained it was the rim of an old volcano. Nick also described that the island of Santorini is part of a dormant but active volcano.

After thanking George and accepting their luggage, along with fruit and champagne, Nick and Anna decided to order dinner to the suite so they could continue to enjoy the impressive view and forthcoming sunset. Nick and Anna clinked glasses and toasted to a successful filming. They discussed some of the details of what was expected during the week. Nick didn't go into much detail about the players on the show only that everyone had arrived two days ago and were supposed to be enjoying the island to get in the mood for Monday's filming. In the morning, Nick would head down to the beach where they would be filming the first segment. He invited Anna to watch. Anna thought it would be exciting to see and accepted. The following morning would bring Anna into Nick's world of reality television.

TEN

In the morning, Steven and a crewmember picked up Nick and Anna. They drove the length of the island passing restaurants that lined the road every few hundred feet, and arrived to a somewhat secluded beach with one hotel perched beachside. Part of the beach had been roped off to create a staging area.

They parked along the road and made their way toward the beach. Anna looked over to the roped-off area noticing chairs under thatched umbrellas that provided a shady place for the participants. The chairs appeared to be made of seagrass, grouped in sets of two, and set perpendicular to the ocean. A walkway made of weathered wood connected the beach to the hotel patio. Anna's eyes were drawn to the large rectangular swimming pool adjacent to the terrace. This pool was nearly three times the length of the pool at their hotel and was tastefully decorated with luscious greenery in potted plants. The group was forced to walk poolside to make their way to the terrace connected to the hotel lobby. Large glass windows separated the courtyard from the hotel's grand entrance.

Anna was led through the patio entrance into the lobby and told she would be able to watch the show unfold from there. Nick and Steven left Anna, promising to check on her later. She wasn't introduced to the others who were already seated in the makeshift green room, so she took a seat on a cushioned chair.

Anna was relieved the weather was milder today, and the contestants wouldn't be sitting around in bikinis and banana hammocks. She eyed the guest seated across from her. The woman had strawberry-blonde shoulder-length hair and wore a peach cardigan with a silky flower-printed skirt that settled just below her kneecaps. The woman was immersed in a magazine and didn't look up. Next to her, the man in khaki pants and a polo shirt stared at his phone screen.

Anna scanned the room and noticed a mocha-skinned man standing near the refreshments. He was dressed in a pale linen shirt and brown slacks with leather loafers on his feet. His eyes were a deep chocolate brown, and his face had sharp cheekbones, accentuated by thick dreadlocks pulled back into a low ponytail. He smiled at Anna, and his white teeth gleamed against the contrast of his dark smooth face. He was quite stunning. Anna could make out a full muscular chest under his shirt. A gold chain hung around his neck, his shirt hiding what talisman might be attached. He held a coffee in his hand and gestured to Anna, asking if she'd like a cup. Anna got up and approached the table where he stood.

"Hi, I'm Anna. That coffee looks really good right about now. I guess there's a long day ahead." She reached out to shake hands. He moved his coffee to accept Anna's handshake.

"Hi Anna, I'm Mike. The coffee helps with the jet lag. I think that's been the toughest but," he took a sip of the coffee he held, swallowed, and continued, "since they flew me in two days ago, I'm starting to adjust."

Mike had an American accent. Anna wasn't surprised. Most of the contestants on Nick's shows were American. Only recently did he talk about trying to get international players. Even though the show was supposed to be reality-based, Nick referred to the people on his show as players. "Players in the game of life," he would say. Human interaction fascinated Nick and Anna. Part of the reason he loved what he did was to see the mess of social psychology unfold.

Anna poured herself a cup of coffee, adding some cream. "So, Mike, are we allowed to talk about why we're here?" Anna asked, pretending she didn't know why they were, in fact, there. The idea, as Nick had explained earlier, was to get players on the show without divulging exactly who had requested their presence. He wanted to get genuine reactions when the guests met face to face with the person who considered them to be their true love.

"If I could tell you, I would." Mike let out a chuckle. "It's crazy to think I get flown halfway across the globe based on being told," he deepened his voice to mimic who he spoke with from the show, "'someone who was once important to you wants to see you again.'" Returning to his regular voice, he asked, "Does that make me seem desperate?"

"Not really. No. Who wouldn't want to find out who still cares about them? It doesn't necessarily mean it will work out. But to know someone feels that strongly about you. That they would apply to be on a reality television show. Well, that makes it appealing, either way, to take the chance." Anna blew on her coffee cup before taking a sip.

"And a free trip to this gorgeous island is totally worth it! So, is it the same for you then, Anna? Some guy, or gal, has been pining away for you?"

Anna didn't want to deceive Mike. "Well, actually, my husband is the producer," she supplied somewhat guiltily. She felt terrible that she wasn't in the same boat as Mike. "This trip is a bit of a getaway for us, when he's not working. I've actually never had the chance to watch a show filming, so he's put me back here to see how it all goes on."

Mike raised his eyebrows as if contemplating something, but said nothing. He looked past Anna at the two other players who were seated on a loveseat. He mentally noted one man and one woman. "Sixty-six percent," Mike uttered under his breath. "What's that?" Anna asked.

"By the ratio here, it would appear more women are willing to search for a lost love than men. Men will probably just go on and try to live a life that they think is satisfying."

"Oh, I'm not so sure about that. This is just a small sample of the whole population. Do you really think it would always turn out that way?"

"Well, I'm here because I obviously didn't try to fix a relationship that could have been the real deal."

"Do you have any idea who is waiting for you out there?"

"I actually feel pretty confident that I do. I'll be blown away if it's not who I think it is. And if it's not who I think it is, I'm afraid I'm going to break their heart because my heart has been taken for quite a while."

Anna wasn't sure if she should press him for more, but she was intrigued. Mike went on, "I think back to how it ended, and I can't believe I didn't fight for her to stay. I guess I was just stubborn. I didn't want to compromise, make concessions, so she left. I didn't blame her, really. But I was angry and needed time to cool off. And by then, she seemed to have moved on. So I let it go. I let her go."

"What kind of compromise weren't you willing to make? If you don't mind my asking."

"I'll try to make it a short story," Mike sipped his coffee. "We were living together in Boston. Both working, trying to get our careers started, in our twenties, fearless, our whole lives ahead of us. I was honest with her that I never want to get married. My parents had divorced, and I saw the breakdown of that marriage, the fighting and the bickering turning into mistrust and infidelity. I split time with my parents, spending every other weekend with one then the other. And they would talk about each other. Not just talk, complain. I said to myself I would never put myself in that situation. So I thought we were both on the same page. Enjoying our time together but no need to talk about marriage." He shook his head then added, "Why does everyone need to be married to have a loving, respectful relationship?" Anna pursed her lips, not answering his rhetorical question. He brushed at his linen slacks then continued. "Well, eventually, we started to talk about it. Talking about it turned to arguing about it. She said she felt like she was wasting her time if it wasn't going to lead to anything more. What more she wanted, I couldn't figure out. We had been happy." Mike looked down into his coffee as if searching for the answer. Then he shrugged and looked up to meet Anna's face. "Eventually, she moved to L.A., and I didn't chase her. She had a career opportunity, and I was done feeling pressured to change my mind. So that's how it ended. I've tried to move on, dating, but no one has sparked in me what I felt when I was with her. I'm still not sure the issue is resolved, but I know that I don't want to be without her. And if it's not her, well, all of this has got me thinking I need to find out if there is a chance for us to work things out. We've kept in touch loosely on Facebook, and I'll admit I've been a coward. I could have tried to rekindle something."

"How long has it been since she moved away?"

"Almost two and a half years." Mike looked down at the drink in his hand. "I know. That's a long time to hold a flame for someone. But I really didn't have a choice. The heart knows what it wants. It just takes time for the brain to follow and figure it out."

Anna was almost speechless. Here she was married three years, and her husband's dedication to work was her biggest problem. Well, she hoped that was her biggest problem. She still had a niggling feeling in the back of her head that she was missing something. Were the late-night work sessions, dinners out, and phone calls all work-related, or was there something more going on? Nick still showed her affection when they were together, but there was an awful lot of time when they weren't together.

Mike gestured towards the doorway. "If you're really trying to see what's going on with the show, you should stand over there." As Anna started to get up, a handler walked in to escort the three contestants into a room off of the lobby. He then asked Anna to follow him. She was brought to an outdoor seating area under a large wooden pergola draped in pink flowers. She had a view of the swimming pool with the wooden boardwalk leading to the beach where all the action would take place. Anna saw Steven and Nick talking. There were a handful of people milling around. Three people were seated in chairs, evenly spaced apart, an empty chair between them.

Ah, these must be the courageous lovelorn participants, Anna thought. She watched Nick walk up to a woman in one of the contestant chairs. He leaned over her, putting his hand on her shoulder. He spoke with her, but Anna was too far away to hear what was said. Anna stood from her seated position and slowly walked down the boardwalk, hoping to get into ear-shot. As she neared the staging area, she had a better view of the contestants. She focused on the woman Nick had been speaking with. The woman's hair was pulled to one side, and the rest of the golden hair cas-caded down one shoulder. She looked in Anna's dir-ection with severe eyes and pursed lips. She looked nervous. She was twisting her hands in her lap while looking at Anna. Recognition dawned on Anna. Cindy, Nick's assistant producer, sat in a contestant chair. But why?

Suddenly Nick's face was blocking Anna's view of Cynthia. He approached Anna and was saying some-thing, but Anna's brain wouldn't work to make sense of his words.

"What?" she asked. Nick started to guide Anna to a seat away from the stage.

"What are you doing over here?" he asked. "I thought you'd watch from the hotel."

"I...I couldn't hear anything, so I was coming closer to hear the show."

"Cam should have brought you an earpiece." Nick looked nervous, too.

Steven rushed over to intercede. "Anna, let's get you a seat a bit farther away from the fire." He laughed, a bit awkwardly and looked over at Nick and then back at Cindy as he ushered Anna up the boardwalk toward the hotel. "Nick, you'll be needed. I'll get Anna squared away," Steven called over his shoulder, leaving Nick watching them walk away. Ahead of them was the handler who escorted Anna outside. "Cam, I need a headset for Anna, here," Steven directed him. Anna was back under the shade of the pergola, and Steven informed her Cam will bring over the headset, and he'll get her something to drink. Anna tried to make sense of everything she'd seen and heard: Cynthia in a contestant's chair; Nick, Steven, and Cynthia looking nervous; Nick reassuring Cynthia; Nick inviting Anna to come on this trip. Why this trip? He'd never invited her to a work filming before.

Cam interrupted Anna's thoughts as he handed her a headset. He demonstrated how to turn it on and adjust the volume. A hotel staff member approached, placing a tall champagne glass in front of Anna. "A mimosa from Mr. Hughes," he explained. She thanked him and took a long gulp. The cool liquid calmed her nerves. She drank more of the refreshing beverage and slipped the earpiece into her ear. At first, all she could hear was the crash of the ocean waves, and then she listened to the voice of the show host. It only took her a moment to recognize the voice as Nick's.

Nick?

She squinted to see Nick standing on the beach in front of a camera. He was welcoming everyone to the first episode of "True Loves." Anna had no idea Nick was going to be on the show.

Why wouldn't he have told me that?

She tried to focus on what Nick was saying. He was explaining that the first contestant is essential to him.

What? Anna couldn't believe what she was hearing.

He was introducing Cynthia. Anna couldn't breathe. She gasped for air, trying to slow her breathing and focus. She never thought of Nick as mendacious. Could he have been deceiving her this whole time? Did he bring her here to break up with her? How long? Is this affair with Cynthia the first, or were there others that Anna was blind to? Her mind swirled with scenarios, replaying Nick's long absences and plans unfulfilled.

Anna took another big gulp of the champagne mixed with juice, finishing the glass. Gaining confidence from the alcohol swirling in her head, she ripped the earpiece out and pushed back from the table, rising to her feet. She boldly marched down the boardwalk, saying Nick's name. "Nick! Nick!" She finally got his attention and just about everyone else on the beach. Onlookers crowded onto the boardwalk to get a better view of the commotion. Nick turned away from the camera to watch Anna come barreling down the beach toward him.

"How could you?" She shouted at him, "How could you humiliate me like this. Bringing me here to announce you've found the love of your life!" She clenched her fists as they walked towards each other.

Nick said something to the cameraman and then reached out to take her by the arm while saying, "Anna, not here."

She yanked her arm backward, stepping back out of his reach, tripping on a board, which sent her sprawling onto her backside. Nick reached down to help her up, but Anna jerked away, scooted backward then crawled to her feet. "No, not here, Nick," Anna hissed the words vehemently and turned to walk away.

Nick started to call her name, but Steven stopped him. "Let her go. I'll go talk to her. I'm not sure how you're going to smooth this over."

Anna pushed her way through the small crowd that had gathered and headed into the lobby of the hotel. Steven entered the hall after her while speaking into his headset. "Keep rolling. Anna," he called across the lobby floor. "Where are you going? Come sit down with me."

Anna paced, her sandals clicking on the marble floor. "I...I just have to go. I need to get off this island. I can't be here." Her voice caught in her throat, and hot tears leaked from her eyes. "Did you know?" she whispered.

Steven didn't answer her question. Instead, he said, "You need to keep watching the show."

"Are you crazy?" Anger started to bubble to the surface again. "I need to leave." *I don't want to see Nick profess his love to her.*

"Anna, will you wait to talk with Nick? I can promise you will feel better if you watch the show. Please trust me. You know I love you and Nick. He's fucked up. I can't deny that, but you really need to watch. Come sit outside with me".

"I...I can't. I can't go back out there in front of all those people. He invited all those people, all the viewers, into our life. I have to go. Please get me a car back to my hotel. I just can't be here right now."

Resigned, Steven called for a car. When the vehicle arrived, he held the door open for Anna to climb in. "Just keep an open mind, Anna. Nick loves you. Give him a chance to explain."

"I can't make any promises." Anna pushed her palm against her chest as if trying to stop her heart from aching. "I have to get out of here." She pulled the car door closed.

Anna felt exhausted. Mentally and emotionally drained. She kept playing over and over again in her head the signs she had missed. Well, she hadn't really missed them all, had she? She was concerned, but she didn't want to believe the worst, so she let it go. She felt foolish.

Sheer adrenaline got Anna through packing her bags and arranging the next flight from the island to Athens. She had a full two weeks off from work. She didn't want to go home. She didn't want to make it easy for Nick to find her and try to assuage his guilt. He would probably be happy to know she left. Making it easier on him. She'll deal with the logistics of breaking up later. Right now, she just needed time away from their home, not to be reminded of him everywhere she looked.

ELEVEN

She dozed on the short flight to Athens. When she arrived and powered her phone back on, she saw she had missed two calls from Nick and one from Steven. "Bastards," she muttered. A fourth missed call was Lauren. She still hadn't decided where she would go from Athens. Anywhere but home is all she knew. So she found a seat at a charging station in the airport and called Lauren.

After explaining the fiasco to Lauren and fighting back the urge to scream and cry, they hatched a plan. Lauren urged Anna to surround herself with loved ones. Lauren pointed out that she was one of them, so she would take off some time and meet Anna wherever she chose.

Anna pictured her childhood home in Connecticut. While she knew it would be easy to hole up there, Anna didn't want to go to her parents. At the moment, she was embarrassed and didn't want to explain the situation to them. Anna couldn't imagine them understanding, having just celebrated their

40th wedding anniversary last year.

She thought about her brother, Josh. She knew Josh would be on her side, even though Josh and Nick got along like brothers. Josh spoke more frequently with Nick than with her. The two grown men entered various fantasy leagues together throughout the year, always a friendly bet, the winner usually getting a commemorative tee shirt or a bottle of wine. She shook her head as if the action would shake the memories from her mind.

Anna decided Josh's place in Charlotte would be cathartic. Anna had only visited her brother once, a decade ago, when he moved from Chapel Hill to Charlotte. He had stayed with her in Santa Monica about four years ago, but their annual reunion was in Connecticut. Their parents insisted on family gatherings at the holidays, whether Christmas time or the fourth of July. Anna preferred to visit at Christmas. Although there wasn't always a promise of snow, Anna liked the reprieve from the warm California winter. Sometimes they would plan a New Year's visit and head to northern New England for snow and skiing.

Anna hoped her visit to Josh wouldn't be an imposition. She wanted to stay with him for a few days to sift through her emotions and prepare for the inevitable conversation with Nick.

She called his number and exhaled audibly as she waited for the call to connect. She didn't go into specifics on the phone, telling him she would explain in person and that she needed to be around family right now. Thankfully, he was happy to have her and planned to pick her up at the airport.

The next possible flight would be in the morning. Anna texted Josh the information and went about finding a nearby hotel for the night. She grabbed a cab and, once at the hotel, checked in, leaving her bag with reception, then headed straight to the bar to wait for her room.

She pretended to read but couldn't concentrate on her book.

Leaving her drink, she went to the ladies room to splash water on her face. Looking in the mirror, she asked herself how it had come to this. Her eyes welled with tears, and grief over her dismantled marriage bombarded her. A noise she didn't recognize escaped her lips, her body convulsed with deep, gut-wrenching sobs. She ran into a stall, turning the lock quickly, and heaved the contents of her stomach into the toilet. Not her most graceful moment, she was elated to have been able to keep it together long enough to be alone. She had hoped to be in her hotel room for privacy, but the lobby bathroom was good enough. She heard her phone vibrate in her purse but ignored it to clean herself up, washing her mouth out at the sink. She dabbed her face and neck with a damp towel and used her fingers to comb her hair, pulling it into a ponytail.

Feeling a bit more composed, she decided not to think about Nick, but anger simmered inside her at the mere thought of his name. She clenched and flexed her fingers, taking deep breaths. "Good. I'd rather feel anger toward him than cry over him," she said out loud to her reflection.

With a straight back and determined gait, she headed back to the bar to finish her drink, even though adding alcohol to the situation was not one of her best ideas. Her raw throat reminded her to leave the glass unfinished and sip on water. She looked at her phone and saw that she had missed the text from the hotel, informing her the room was ready.

She made her way to reception, accepted her room key, and headed to the elevator. Once inside her room, she kicked off her shoes and sprawled across the bed. She hadn't realized she'd fallen asleep until a knock on the door awoke her. She held the door open for the bellhop carrying her bag. Anna handed him a few bills as she thanked him on his way out. She closed the door and flopped onto the bed, drifting off again until she woke a few hours later, famished.

Slightly disoriented she squinted at the desk clock and read it was just after eight. Afraid to have another episode similar to the one in the lobby bathroom, Anna ordered room service, showered, and laid out her clothes for her morning flight. She called down to arrange a shuttle for the morning and texted Lauren regarding her flight plans.

She searched the TV for an American movie she could watch to take her mind off of Nick. It was pointless. Her brain wouldn't turn off, and she spent most of the night cursing Nick and his new love, Cynthia. She looked forward to the long international flight to catch up on sleep.

TWELVE

As soon as Anna exited customs, she spotted her big brother wearing his infamous Carolina Blue Tar Heels cap. A smile spread across Josh's face as she approached among the throng of weary travelers. Josh took note of his usually polished sister. She looked spent, her face gaunt where her usually round cheeks would be full with the sun-kissed glow of a southern Californian. When she reached Josh, she gave him a huge hug and he bearhugged her in return.

"Let's get you in the car, and then you can fill me in on exactly why my little sister needed this getaway. Are you hungry? Want to stop for dinner?" Josh led her toward the parking garage.

"I ate on the plane. I honestly would just like to get back to your place, and I'll tell you everything. Thank you for picking me up. You really didn't have to."

"It wasn't a problem. I'm on the early shift this week at the hospital." When they reached Josh's car, he placed her suitcase in the trunk of his blue metallic sedan. "How long are you planning to stay? This is a pretty big bag. And don't think I didn't notice your flight was coming from Athens. Why were you coming from there?"

"My Greek vacation was cut short. I'll get to all that. Tell me what's going on with you?" Josh didn't push Anna to say anymore. He told her he was still a Pharmacist at the Presbyterian Medical Center not far from Cherry, the area where his condominium was located. He bragged he could walk to work, when he wanted, rather than sit in Santa Monica traffic. Anna admitted she was jealous of that fact.

Changing subjects, Josh said, "I hope you have something warm to wear at night in your suitcase. I tend to keep the thermostat low to sleep comfortably."

Anna wrinkled her nose. "I didn't think about that. Can I borrow something of yours tonight and I'll shop tomorrow?"

"Yeah. I'll scrounge up a sweatshirt for you." He kept his eyes on the road as he asked, "When is Lauren getting in? You can borrow my car to get her."

"She'll get in on Thursday night. She's only staying for the weekend."

"You two okay sharing a bed? I only have one spare room. It's a queen-sized bed, though. Otherwise, one of you will have to be on the couch."

"We'll be fine. We've bunked before on our girls trips."

They pulled into the parking area at Josh's condo. They passed the outdoor pool being enjoyed by moms with their young children. Josh's entrance was on the ground floor, making it easy to roll the suitcase into his condo.

Once inside, Josh showed Anna the guest bedroom and placed her bag next to the doorway to the adjoining bathroom. "Let me know what you need. I hung clean towels in the bathroom, and the bedsheets are fresh." He went around to the side of the bed to turn on a lamp. "It's nice to have you here, no matter the circumstance." They left the bedroom, walking back through the living room, and sat at the kitchen island.

"Looks great, Josh." Anna took in the leather furniture, plush carpeting, and an enormous inkblot painting of a horse's head over his mantel. It suited him. "Will Caroline be around?" Anna asked about Josh's girlfriend. They've been dating for several months. Josh had brought Caroline to meet everyone at Christmas in Connecticut. Anna and Caroline hit it off immediately, finding camaraderie in Josh's pitiful previous dalliances.

"I told her you'd be visiting for an unknown amount of time, and I wasn't sure what state of mind you would be in. She'll only be around if you're up for company."

"Josh! That's terrible! You don't have to babysit me. If you want her over, or you want to go out, do it. Do not let me disrupt your entire life!" Anna was exasperated with him. "Seriously, you men are all crazy. I don't understand how you treat people you care about...." Anna suddenly stopped what she was saying and changed direction. "Got any wine? I'm ready to tell you why I'm here."

Two hours and a bottle and a half later, Josh was up to speed on the "Catastrophe of Santorini" as they now referred to it. There had been tears, on Anna's part, and laughter, on Josh's, which he apologized for. It seemed so ridiculous to him. He just couldn't believe Nick would do that to Anna. Maybe Nick had gotten so caught up in the show business that he lost sight of what was important. People made mistakes. Josh assured Anna that Nick would be begging her to take him back. Anna wasn't so sure. She pointed out that the show was called "True Loves" and Nick and Cindy looked very nervous with Anna there. Nick introduced Cynthia as someone *essential* to him. Anna remembered that Steven had said Nick messed up. Actually, "fucked up" were the words he used. If Steven admitted Nick messed up, then it was definitely grim.

Josh wanted to tell Anna things would be better in the morning, but he knew that wasn't the truth. "Try to get some sleep," he told her. He held up the bottle of wine they had been sharing. "Do you want any more of this?"

"No, thanks. I'm already a wreck. I'll take some water with me to bed." She took the bottle of water he offered and blew him a kiss goodnight. "Thanks. For everything."

"Any time," he winced as the words left his mouth. "You know what I mean. I'm here for you, any time, not just when you're life's crap."

"Gee, thanks. You make a sister feel loved." Anna

closed the door to her temporary bedroom. Josh watched the door until the light went out.

He was fuming. He didn't want to add to Anna's worries, but he was going to strangle Nick when he got the chance. "What the hell?" Josh put his head in his hands. He knew he should go to bed, but first, he had a phone call to make. It was four o'clock in the morning in Greece, and Josh didn't give a fuck if he woke the bastard up.

THIRTEEN

When Anna woke Wednesday morning, she felt better. Not about her situation, but she actually slept through the night. She followed the sound of clinking dishes to the kitchen.

"Morning," Josh greeted her. "Coffee or OJ?" He continued to put dishes away as he unloaded the dishwasher. "If you get dressed, you can drop me at work and use the car today."

"Coffee, please," she walked to the counter and took a mug from the cabinet. "I will get dressed *tout suite*." She poured half a cup and asked, "Do you have cream or milk for this?" Josh opened the refrigerator and handed Anna the cream. Anna added some to her cup then sat at the kitchen island while Josh closed the dishwasher.

He picked up his own cup, taking a sip. "What do you have on the docket for today?" He asked her. He wasn't ready to divulge that he had spoken with Nick the night before.

"Shopping, of course. Retail therapy is the best

kind," Anna supplied. Anna asked him more about Caroline, and if they wanted to have dinner together.

"I'll ask her and let you know. Are you up for going out, or should we cook in?"

"I'm fine with whatever." Then changing her mind, "No, I would like to cook for you. It'll give me something to do and keep my mind occupied." She put her empty cup in the sink and hurried to her room to get dressed. She grabbed her purse and headed out with Josh.

After dropping him at work, she had time to plan a menu for tonight's dinner before shops would open. She sat in the parked car, using her phone to search for recipes. Her screen lit up with an incoming call. Nick. Her hand started to shake looking at his name on the screen. She didn't want to talk to him. The hurt was still fresh, she wasn't ready. She swiped down, sending the call to voicemail and let the tears flow.

Once she was able to compose herself she continued searching for a meal that would take time to prepare. She settled on seafood paella, a dish traditionally made with saffron, rice, shrimp, mussels, Spanish chorizo sausage, and chicken. Anna made a list of the groceries she would need to purchase later and estimated an hour to put the meal together. She decided to make an additional stop to buy some Rioja Spanish wine. She took her time researching where the best local shopping would be and headed that way.

She parked on East Boulevard, and meandered the street looking in the shop windows. She followed her phone's GPS to several women's clothing stores. Taking her time in each shop, Anna purchased a silk tank top and a pair of white jeans. She also found an electric blue bomber jacket she couldn't resist. Anna typically wouldn't wear something so vibrant. She hated to attract unwanted attention and kept her wardrobe to primarily calming colors or black. But she figured *what the hell, need to change things up* and bought it before she could change her mind.

Anna hadn't given thought to how long she would stay with Josh. She hoped she'd be ready to return to Santa Monica with Lauren after the weekend. She knew she couldn't avoid Nick forever. The business of breaking up would have to be dealt with eventually. She supposed he would move out since he would have somewhere to go, with *Cindy*. Just thinking the woman's name made her cringe. Then she'd have to figure out if they would put the house on the market. Anna tried not to think about all the decisions that would have to be made in the coming weeks.

She took her time the remainder of the morning window-shopping. Josh texted her around lunchtime to let her know Caroline would be joining them for dinner. He asked Anna to pick him up at four o'clock. She stopped in a café for lunch and went about picking up what she needed for the evening's dinner. After unpacking the groceries at Josh's, it was time to pick him up. She mused the day went by quickly when she kept herself busy.

At six, Caroline walked into the condo to Anna fully engaged in cooking the paella. She was cursing herself for making everything from scratch. Usually, she would have purchased some yellow rice, but wanting to keep her mind off of Nick, she decided to buy saffron and the herbs and spices to create as authentic a Spanish dish as possible. It wasn't the most challenging dish, just time-consuming. She needed to attend the stove, stirring the rice in the paella broth.

She gave Caroline a quick one-handed hug, the wooden spoon in motion with the other hand. In one long breath, she told Caroline she and Nick were breaking up. Nick wanted to be with someone else, and there was nothing for her to do, but accept it. Caroline looked at Josh then back to Anna with concern in her eyes. "Oh, please don't pity me. I will be fine. Once my heart heals, I'll move on. He certainly has," Anna emphatically stated. "Ugh, I am so angry with him. I just don't understand why he would take me with him to the show taping. Why humiliate me in front of an audience? Why not just tell me at home, or let me watch the show and find out later?"

"Oh, Anna, the show wouldn't come out for months. That wouldn't be practical," Caroline supplied. Josh and Anna gave her an incredulous look. Then Anna burst out laughing.

"I'm glad you can laugh about it." Josh cracked a smile, too.

Once Anna composed herself, she added, "The whole thing is so ridiculous I have to laugh, or I'll cry, *again*. But you're right, Caroline. It wouldn't make sense for him to wait until the show aired. He obviously wanted to get it done as soon as possible. Why not tell me before filming the show, then? He could have been done with me, free and clear by the time they started taping. I just can't wrap my brain around how he chose to break my heart. It wasn't kind, and I never thought of Nick as malicious. Well, clearly, I didn't know him like I thought I did." It was hard for Anna to keep her mind from thinking about all the incredible times they had, the sexual chemistry, the daily banter that was unique to them. She thought she knew all his quirks and what made him tick.

Anna chastised herself for being so naive, thinking she could have the fairy tale. How would she ever let him go? Her heart ached, thinking of a life without Nick. *Time heals all.* Isn't that the expression? She just needs time to get over him and the life they shared. Anna felt her eyes start to tear so she wiped at the edges with one hand and turned her back to hide her face.

"Josh, could you set the table and Caroline will you open the wine on the table. Dinner is ready. I'll plate it and bring it over."

With a loaf of bread on the table and wine in their glasses, the Spanish-themed meal was enjoyed immensely. Caroline was practically humming during each bite she took. Josh chuckled and looked at Anna as if to communicate telepathically, "She does this, it's a compliment."

Anna could only imagine what other times Caroline hummed. They both laughed, and Caroline looked up at them. "What?"

Anna and Josh put on sober faces and said in unison,

"Nothing."

After dinner, Josh and Caroline cleared the dishes and joined Anna in the living room. Anna had settled into an armchair leaving the love seat for her brother and Caroline. As they walked from the kitchen towards the couch, Caroline and Josh exchanged a look that Anna wouldn't have given a second thought except that Caroline's eyes were getting bigger by the second.

"Please tell me what's going on before Caroline's eyes fall out of their sockets."

"Oh, you caught that," Josh frowned at Caroline. "Good, you're already sitting down." Josh sat on the edge of the loveseat.

Instead of joining him, Caroline said, "I should go and leave you two alone now."

"Wait a second, Caroline." Josh turned to his sister. "Anna, Caroline knows what's going on with you and Nick. And not just what you told her tonight. I had to talk to someone before I tell you what Nick said."

Anna swallowed audibly. "What do you mean, 'what Nick said'? And I realize you and Caroline would talk." Turning to Caroline with a pleading look, Anna said, "Caroline, please stay. I have nothing to hide and I think I'll need more emotional support if what Josh is telling me is from Nick." Anna shook her head rolling her eyes to the ceiling. "Do I even want to hear this?"

Josh started, "I was pissed after you told me what he did on the island. I called him last night. And before you berate me for sticking my nose into your business, remember, you showed up on *my* doorstep. *You* involved me. Nick and I are friends, but you know I will always look out for you - unless you fuck up."

"Understood." Anna buried her face in her hands, peeking through her fingers at Josh. "So what did Nick have to say? Did he make excuses for-"

Josh cut her off. "Slow down. Some of what he said didn't make sense, and I told him that. He admitted to messing up. He said, and I quote, 'My mouth's writing checks my body can't cash.' He also used the friend card, saying if we were ever really friends, then I would know he would never cheat on you."

"Let's pretend he hadn't officially cheated on me. I heard with my own two ears, he was going to be on True Loves with Cynthia."

Stopping Anna from refuting anything else he was saying, Josh continued, "Nick asked- pleaded, really- to have you watch the recording of the show. He seemed to think it would clear things up."

"Oh, God. Why would I want to watch it and relive the humiliation again? It won't come out for weeks, if not months. I have to get back to some semblance of my life."

"No, not the aired episode. Nick said he would send me the cut he has. Apparently, he knows you well enough that you might never look at it if it came directly from him. He said he was glad you were with me...since you aren't answering his calls." Josh looked at Caroline, then met Anna's eyes. "He sent it today. We can play it on my laptop if you think you're ready."

Anna took a few deep breaths. Her hands were shaking, so she clasped them together. She couldn't decide if she was angry with her brother for contacting Nick without speaking to her first, or if she was still reacting to Nick's betrayal.

"I'm not ready. Maybe when Lauren gets here tomorrow. I can't watch it tonight." She left the room without another word. Afraid if she spoke over the lump in her throat, the hurt she was holding in would bubble over into unkind words for her meddling brother, when in fact, she needed to channel this upset to the person responsible for it. Nick.

FOURTEEN

he next morning Josh was gone before Anna woke. He left her a note on the kitchen island.

Sorry how things ended last night. I'll be home around 4:30pm. We can pick up Lauren together, if you want. Love you.

Your overprotective brother

He had left the car keys next to the note. Anna didn't feel like going out. She briefly looked at the coffee maker and decided to go back to bed. She didn't want to think about Nick or the video clip. She wanted to slide back into a dreamless sleep.

After sleeping a few more hours, Anna finally decided she couldn't have a pity party any longer. She showered and dressed and decided to go for a walk to clear her head. The hurt was still ever-present and she only had to think Nick's name for her throat to feel like it was filled with a chunk of coal she couldn't swallow. How can she move on when her love for him felt like her entire world? She tried to remind herself of all the times she felt let down by Nick, thinking that would make her fall out of love with him. All it did was make her realize how much she cared about him. If she hadn't cared, all the delayed flights and late work meetings wouldn't have bothered her.

It was a brilliant day outside, the sun shining brightly contrasted to Anna's dark mood. She stopped to feel the sun's warmth on her face then unzipped her new bright blue jacket, its bold color hiding her shattered insides. The street was lined with vibrant green trees and a rainbow of blossoms. Everywhere Anna looked shouted life and vitality while she felt like her life was decaying.

A few blocks away from Josh's complex, she spotted a coffee shop. Her stomach growled to remind her she hadn't eaten yet. She entered the door with the familiar green mermaid etched on the glass and felt a cold blast of air hit her face. Suddenly feeling chilled, she zipped her jacket and walked up to the counter. After ordering, she sat at a small table by the window to wait for her food and coffee. She was reminded of the time she met Mark Williams for coffee. She remembered the excitement of seeing him and cursed under her breath when she also remembered that she had introduced him to her best friend. For a moment, she had felt a glimmer of hope; that after Nick, she could move on. Of course, the only other person to whom she was attracted, she pushed onto her friend to keep herself from straying!

After her leisurely brunch, Anna walked back to Josh's place. She decided to check in with work and let them know she planned to return the following week. Anna effortlessly wasted hours checking social media, something she had deliberately stayed away from, for fear she might see a post from Nick that would have her in tears. Thankfully, he hadn't posted anything. She closed down Josh's computer and decided to walk to the medical center to meet Josh for his walk home.

***

"He's a rat bastard," Lauren held her drink into the air for emphasis. An empty bottle of wine sat in the kitchen, and a second open bottle rested on the coffee table between the women. Josh ransacked his cabinets looking for crackers, olives, and cheese—*something*- to feed the women who were indulging in their second, maybe third, glass of wine. He wasn't precisely counting, but now tongues were loosened, and nothing was being held back. His sister seemed to be in better spirits with her friend's company.

"Lauren, I *married* him. What does that make me?"

"He's a deceptive, squirming, slimy snake. He fooled us all. Right, Josh? You were friends with him! He had you fooled, too!" Lauren turned quickly, and wine sloshed over the edge of her glass. Josh grabbed a roll of paper towels, carrying it in with some crackers and cheese.

"We are friends. That's why I'm willing to give him some benefit of the doubt. Not a ton, mind you, but some. They say there are two sides to every story." Lauren and Anna raised their eyebrows and glared in unison at him.

It felt good to have her people around her. Beth chimed in via face time. "I just can't believe it. You two were so in love. It just doesn't make sense. Who is this, Cynthia, anyway?"

Lauren wanted to jump through the tablet screen and tell her friend to shut-up. She loved Beth, but too often, Beth's heart of gold only saw the good in people. It made Beth gullible at times.

"This isn't the time to make sense of things. It's time to bash Nick for being an ass!" Lauren blurted. "It doesn't matter *who* this woman is. It only matters that he get an ass-kicking for being a conniving, two-timing, weasel. Who does that? If things aren't right in a relationship, you talk about it! Then if it can't be fixed, you go your separate ways. You don't take someone on a romantic trip to break the news you're in love with someone else! It takes time to fall in love. There must have been plenty of time to tell Anna he had feelings for someone else."

Anna loved her girlfriends for supporting her without question. It felt good to name call. But when all was said and done, Anna felt a loss. A gaping hole in her chest where her heart used to reside.

What Lauren didn't realize was that it didn't necessarily take time to fall in love. Sometimes it's that first moment you meet someone you know they are meant to be part of your life forever.

That's how Anna felt the first time she laid eyes on Nick. It seemed like yesterday when they bumped into each other at a fundraiser. She had clumsily whacked his arm while animating a story to an associate. She couldn't take her eyes off of him, and thankfully he asked if he could call her. The rest was, as they say, history.

She thought that was how he felt, too. Inevitably you can be attracted to multiple people. For Christ's sake, she was enticed by her brother's friend, who just happened to walk back into her life while all this was happening. Plenty of people find love more than once in their life. But when you find that connection, don't you fight for it? There's a reason you say 'I do' to one person. You are saying I don't to the rest of the world. You put that one person above all others. Do you let another person get into your marriage? Not unless something is making you unhappy. Was Nick unhappy? There wasn't any emotional or physical abuse. They weren't bored of each other, Anna thought. They made each other laugh, had their own private jokes. Was it neglect? Anna didn't believe she neglected, Nick.

On the contrary, he was usually the one with the busier schedule that interfered with nurturing their relationship. Maybe that's why Mark Williams became so tempting. Anna was feeling lonely. Could Nick have been feeling that way, too, and he took it to the next level? Spending more time with his colleague – she couldn't bear to use her name - than his own wife, he began to feel like she was the right person for him instead of Anna.

Her mind began to spin with all the possibilities of how it could have happened. The most frustrating part was that it was entirely out of her control. She couldn't control Nick anymore than he could control her. They each made decisions every day to be faithful or not. Anna believed she had treasured their marriage. She had treasured Nick. Now the treasure box had been looted. There was nothing left inside, not even a remnant of something sparkly or shiny.

There's nothing left to be done but let him go.

Anna was snapped out of her reverie when a fork clanged in the kitchen sink. She waited for Josh and Lauren to finish their commentary. "Hey, guys, while I would love to continue this mope fest, I'm ready to watch the video."

Josh cleared his throat. "You sure?"

"No. I don't know if I'll ever be, but I don't want this.... this *mourning* of my marriage, to go on forever. I've got to find a way to move on, so let's watch whatever crap he's sent so I can put it behind me. It'll probably piss me off all over again, but I'd rather do it now than have it blindside me in a few months when it airs."

Josh placed his laptop on the coffee table in front of Anna. Lauren came around and sat next to her, holding the phone so Beth could see as well. Josh pressed and swiped until his screen filled with black. Lauren entwined her fingers with Anna's. The only sound heard was the hum of the video playing. Then the screen filled with Nick's face introducing the audience to "True Loves." Josh tapped the volume button several times, filling the room with Nick's voice.

"Welcome to the first episode of True Loves. The reality show where contestants have a chance to rekindle romance with someone from their past. Perhaps it's someone they only met in passing- that person that got away. Perhaps it's a previous lover that walked away. No matter how well they knew each other, this is the chance for them to find out if, in fact, they are....true loves." While Nick spoke, the camera had panned on the three contestants. One man and two women sat in rattan chairs on the beach. The camera paused on each one as Nick spoke. The broad smile on Cynthia's face was incongruent to her jittery hands twisting in her lap.

"That's Cynthia!" Anna pointed at the screen when the camera had stopped on her. "Do you see how nervous she is?"

No one responded, mesmerized by the drama unfolding.

The camera was back on Nick. "Let's meet our first participant, Cynthia. I don't know what I would do without her. Cynthia is an essential part of this very show as our assistant producer. She has worked tirelessly to make this show a reality, pun intended –"

Off-camera we can hear Nick's name being called. It's Anna. Nick has turned toward her, confused. He turns back to the camera and says, "Stop rolling." But the camera keeps filming.

Lauren, Beth, Josh, and Anna watch as Anna screams at Nick. Nick doesn't get a word in other than "Anna, not here." Then, Steven is following Anna up the boardwalk towards the hotel. Nick is looking at the camera again, his face forlorn. He touches his ear and then appears to snap out of it. He smiles at the camera and continues.

"Let's meet our first participant. Assistant producer to the show, Cynthia has been committed to the idea of this show." Turning to Cynthia, he continues, "Cynthia, tell us what brings you here." Cynthia's voice cracks, and she clears her throat. "There is a man I deeply care about, and I was foolish enough to push him out of my life two years ago. When we started developing this show, I knew I had to track him down." Cynthia takes a deep breath. "Mike and I were together for several years after graduating college. He didn't want to get married, and I kept pushing him. I'm here today to tell him I don't need to get married. I just want to be with him."

"Are you ready to tell this to Mike?" Nick asks with a serious expression on his face.

Cynthia responds with just as serious an expression. "I know there are many possibilities how this could end. He could be with someone else and completely over me. I've prepared myself for that. I need to find out if there is any possibility for us to rekindle what we had." She laughs lightly, "So, to answer your question, yes, I'm ready to tell this to Mike."

The camera focuses on the boardwalk, and a tall mocha-skinned man is walking calmly towards the beach. As he gets closer, his steps become hurried. The moment Mike recognizes Cynthia, his face lights up like a firework in the night. He shakes his head, smiling, as she stands before him. He grabs her in a hug lifting her off the ground, burying his face in her hair. His microphone picks up his muffled words. "Thank god, it's you! It's been too long." They separate their faces but keep holding each other, staring into one another's eyes with big goofy grins on their faces.

Anna taps the computer pausing the image on the screen. "I met him. Mike. He was waiting to find out who he would be meeting." Anna's words are slow. "I... I don't understand. I...I..." She covers her face in her hands. "Could he have edited the video?"

"Maybe," Josh spoke while looking at the stunned faces on Lauren and Beth. "Should we watch any-more?"

"Let's see where this goes," Lauren finally speaks. "To be honest, Anna, it sounds like you cut Nick off before anything incriminating was even said."

"But, I *heard* him." Anna is pensive for a moment. "I heard him say Cynthia was important to him."

"We heard it, too, Anna. That she's his assistant pro-ducer, important to the show." Beth interjected.

"Oh, God! Did I just blow this completely out of proportion?" Anna looks to each of her friends and brother.

"Anna, I think you need to talk to Nick," Josh offered.

Anna told them she needed to watch it again. They replayed the video from the beginning. They watched Nick as the camera remained on him from the mo-ment Anna walked away to the moment Cynthia had started talking. The camera never cut off of Nick dur-ing Anna's interruption to Cynthia's introduction. It became clear that when he touched his earpiece, he must have been getting a directive to continue with the show. Anna, Lauren, Beth, and Josh continued to watch the recording. They watched Mike hug Cynthia, then holding her hand sit in the chair next to her.

Anna was overwhelmed. She was ecstatic for Mike and Cynthia, and for herself. Anna wanted to cry tears of joy – she was a complete idiot, and her husband wasn't cheating on her. Then she sobered at the realization Nick was going to be furious with her.

She had made an enormous scene, accusing him of infidelity. On national TV! She hadn't returned his calls. She ran away rather than deal with it like an adult. She couldn't even have a rational discussion with the man she loves. Yes, loves. No matter how much she tried to create anger and turn off her feelings, she loves this man, had from the first day they met.

He had every right to be outraged and now she had to plan the biggest apology of her life.

FIFTEEN

Anna moaned as the first rays of light blinded her. She had forgotten to close the drapes last night before getting in bed. Friday morning arrived pounding at her temple. Anna rolled over, searching the nightstand for some ibuprofen. After locating the bottle, she shook out two tablets and gulped them down with some water from the bathroom sink faucet. She turned on the shower and mentally planned her morning.

First thing is first. Get this headache to clear up. Second, call Nick. Lauren doesn't think she should let Nick off the hook too quickly. There are still unanswered questions. If he weren't having an affair with Cynthia, why would Steven say Nick fucked up? Why would Nick admit to her brother that he messed up and *he's writing checks his body can't cash*. What promise was Nick making that he couldn't live up to? Anna knew she had to ask Nick directly. She also had to apologize for her behavior.

Anna showered and dressed before eight o'clock.

She knew Josh would already be gone to work. Lauren had fallen asleep on the couch and apparently hadn't woken during the night to come to bed. Anna used this alone time to telephone Nick. It was just about three in the afternoon in Greece. Anna knew Nick would still be filming, so she wasn't surprised when his voice mail answered her call. She left a message saying she had watched the episode and wanted to talk. Anna hoped to hear from Nick in a few hours and turned her ringer volume to the maximum so she wouldn't miss the call. Her stomach was tied in knots, and she couldn't possibly eat anything, so she decided she would sit with a cup of coffee until Lauren awakes.

Anna sat with her thoughts for a solid thirty minutes before Lauren started to stir. Anna contemplated what she was going to say when Nick returned her call. At least, she hoped he called. She began to imagine him not phoning because he had already reached out several times, and Anna had ignored him. Ouch. She pictured him not returning her calls and felt the pit in her stomach deepen. She had been too angry to realize she was unfair to him.

"Penny for your thoughts," Lauren was sitting up now, with one arm slung over the back of the couch. She turned her head to look at Anna in the kitchen while leaning against the arm of the sofa. "You've been awfully quiet. I've been watching you for a full two minutes."

"That's creepy," Anna joked. "I left Nick a message, and my stomach hurts, waiting for him to return my call."

Lauren got off the couch and walked to sit next to Anna at the kitchen island. "Oh, Anna, he messed up! Nick didn't stop you immediately and explain the error of your thinking. He let you walk away. You're too hard on yourself." Lauren hugged her. "It will all work out. I just know it."

"I'm glad at least someone feels confident about that. I need something to distract me before I have an ulcer from anticipation." Anna turned back to the kitchen island and took another sip of her coffee. "Any developments with our friend Mark Williams?"

Lauren's face began to color. Anna didn't notice at first, but when Lauren shifted uncomfortably in her seat, Anna said, "Spill it!"

Lauren updated Anna on her developing relationship with Mark. So far, they had only been able to meet up once for a late dinner after work, but they had been texting almost daily.

"Did anything *happen* after that late dinner?" Anna probed.

"No. We both had early meetings the next morning. But *I* wanted something to happen!" Lauren admitted. "He is a consummate gentleman. We get along really well, have similar views on a lot of things, and yet we can debate like Bill Gates and Steve Jobs. I wish he wouldn't be such a gentleman, if you know what I mean," she wiggled her eyebrows for emphasis, "but he hasn't had the opportunity not to be. We have plans next weekend when I get back."

"Does he know why you're here visiting me?" Anna

couldn't say why it bothered her to think Mark would know about her marital issues. Really it was no one's business but hers and Nick's.

"I didn't give specifics." Lauren leaned on the kitchen island with her forearms. "Geez, Anna, don't you know me better than that?" Lauren felt insulted at the insinuation, but tried to put herself in Anna's shoes. She could imagine she wouldn't want intimate details of one of her relationships shared. To appease Anna she added, "He couldn't have cared less when I mentioned I was meeting up with you at your brother's place. He simply asked me to pass along a hello to you and your brother. So, um, 'Hi' from Mark." Lauren realized she hadn't mentioned Mark to Anna or Josh. She had wanted to keep him to herself, which was foolish since Josh and Mark were such good friends. They would undoubtedly be sharing time with him.

"I didn't mean anything by it, really, Lauren. I am so utterly embarrassed by this whole situation, and I would be mortified if another person knew what is happening. *I* don't even know what is happening. One moment I'm distraught and heartbroken. Then I realize I've been a fool and could have messed up my marriage with my insecurity."

"Anna, there were a lot of signs that something was off. Maybe he didn't have an affair, but something has not been quite right with you and Nick. You've mentioned it to Beth and me on more than one occasion. You two need to fix whatever is creating a fissure in your marriage- that would lead you to jump to the conclusion that's he's unfaithful."

Anna knew Lauren was right. She needed to apologize to Nick, but she also had to figure out how to align her marriage from veering off-course anymore.

SIXTEEN

DNCE's Cake By The Ocean played loudly from Anna's phone. She immediately recognized the ring tone she had set for Nick's phone number. Lauren held up crossed fingers for good luck and pointed to the guest room, signaling to Anna a place for privacy. Anna hustled into the bedroom, closing the door behind her as she slid her finger along the phone screen to answer his call.

"Nick, thank God, it's you. I am *so* sorry," Anna hiccupped into the phone. Her body betrayed her, despite trying to stay calm, her nerves getting the best of her. She sat balanced on the edge of the bed waiting to hear him speak.

"Anna," Nick sighed her name, relieved to finally hear her voice. "I'm glad you're ready to talk, but I can't believe you wouldn't answer my calls." Anna waited for him to continue. "I had no idea where you were and I was worried…and starting to get angry. If Josh hadn't called, I was about to use a GPS tracker on your phone and report you as a missing person."

Nick let out a soft chuckle, "He really laid into me. You don't ever have to worry that your brother won't stand up for you. He had some choice words and described in detail what he was going to do to me if I had, in fact, cheated on you. And I'd hate to have to pummel him because we get along so well."

Nick cleared his throat and Anna heard the gravitas in his next words. "I just don't understand why you would assume the worst of me? I love you. I would never betray you." Nick waited a beat and then added for levity, "You're stuck with me, babe."

"I love you, too." Anna sniffed as tears streamed down her face. She grabbed tissues from the nightstand and blew her nose. "I was absolutely heartbroken at the thought of you falling in love with Cynthia," she hiccupped, again, "hence, falling out of love with me."

Nick laughed, "I got that. When you screamed it at me in front of a few hundred people. By the way, we edited the show, so our debacle won't be aired. Thank God, I have some pull."

Anna was grateful for that. "Nick, I jumped to a lot of conclusions, and I am sorry for that. I embarrassed us both." Anna rubbed her free hand along the comforter as she took a deep breath and audibly exhaled. "Oh God, Nick. Did this mess up your business? You're not in trouble at work because of me, are you?"

"Babe, you caused quite a lot of drama, which in my business is a good thing. The problem is you didn't have faith in me... faith in us. That's what hurt the most." Nick became quiet.

Anna couldn't take the silent treatment. "Nick, I am sorry I hurt you. I was incensed at the idea of you bringing me to your show to make a public announcement. I was so relieved when I saw the video you sent." A smile played on Anna's lips. "I'm happy for Mike and Cynthia."

"I'm not sure where you got the idea that Cindy and I would hook up."

"The late nights working, showing up with her to our dinner date, the delayed flights, the dinners out with–"

"Stop! Ok, I get it. Wow, I had no idea. Work is intense, and yes, I spend a lot of time with my team-"

"*A lot* of time," Anna interrupted.

"But you knew this when we started dating. Why is it becoming an issue now?"

"I'm not quite sure, Nick," Anna hadn't processed why she was feeling the way she had. "I'll give that some thought *if* you'll give me some answers."

"Go ahead."

"Why did you tell Josh you messed up and something about you writing checks you can't cash? Are our finances in trouble?"

Nick laughed and then sobered. "Well, I had messed up, hadn't I? I let you leave without talking to you. What a fool I was to let you leave that set, knowing what you were thinking was wrong. Look where it got me. My wife ran away from me. I wouldn't have blamed you one bit if there was an ounce of truth, but considering I brought you to the taping, I should have taken better care of you."

"And the check-writing?"

"Ah, right. I believe I said, 'my mouth is writing checks my body can't cash.' And what I mean is that I made a promise to cherish you above all others. You remember that vow, right? Three years isn't that long ago, and I clearly wasn't keeping that promise. For you to jump to that conclusion meant I wasn't giving you what you need. Instead of taking you on a real vacation – vacating our ordinary life – I took you to work. I thought I could kill two birds with one stone. I'm sorry for that."

"Well, aren't we a pair. How much longer will you be shooting?"

"We film an episode a day, so the season should be done in two more weeks, assuming everything goes as planned."

The gears of Anna's brain were turning. Her heart and mind were concocting a plan that she wasn't ready to divulge to Nick. "I'm going to finish my visit with Josh and fly back to LA with Lauren tomorrow. I'll see you home in two weeks?"

"I guess you don't want to come back out here, do you?"

"I can't show my face. Your crew must think I should be locked away in an asylum."

"Nah. Well, maybe. But everyone will get over it."

"I'm afraid *I* won't get over it. I'll see you in Santa Monica. Call me tomorrow?"

"Of course. Enjoy your day, mine's coming to an end. I'm heading to dinner."

"....wiiiith?"

"Steven!" They both laughed.

"Anna," Nick's voice held a serious note, "I hope you'll never doubt my love for you. I know I don't always make the best choices, or make it up to you when I let you down, but I only have eyes for you."

"I'm sorry, Nick." Anna again felt like she had been punched in the gut but for a different reason. She hated the idea of hurting Nick. "I love you so much. I literally went crazy at the idea of you falling out of love with me."

"That could never happen. I told you a long time ago, I had no choice when it came to loving you. I was hooked, and nothing could change that. I probably shouldn't say this out loud."

"Well, now, you have to…"

"If you ever cheated on me, I don't think I could leave you. You might choose to leave me, but I could never leave you. You're like the air I breathe, I can't live without you."

"Well, aren't you overly dramatic?"

"I'm serious. It hurts to think you don't know how deep my feelings are for you. I love you, Anna, more than life itself."

"I love you, too."

After promising to talk tomorrow, they finally said their goodbyes.

Now Anna had work to do.

She and Lauren made plans to be tourists for the day and meet up with Josh and Caroline for dinner at a trendy restaurant in downtown Charlotte. It felt good to not only have finally spoken with Nick but to know what her next steps would be. She didn't want too many people to know her plan, but she also knew she might need help keeping it a secret from Nick, especially if she planned to keep him in the dark for another week and a half. She was nervous, but she knew she deserved to be. Her discomfort was needed to prove to Nick how much he means to her.

Lauren tried to make her feel better by saying anyone would have read the signs similarly and jumped to the same conclusion. At dinner, Anna filled them all in on her plan. The only person with whom she hadn't spoken was the one she needed most, the one person who could make her idea come to fruition. On Sunday, she and Lauren flew back to LA before returning to work on Monday. Anna planned to take a second week off but would work in the interim. She needed at least a week to put her plan into action. And steel her nerves to make it happen.

SEVENTEEN

onday morning, Anna texted Steven.

DO NOT LET NICK SEE THIS! Call me when you are NOT with Nick.

Then she waited.

"What's up, sweetie?" Steven asked as soon as Anna picked up. "Nick told me you finally spoke, and things were cleared up. I wish you had stayed instead of putting a continent between you two."

"Yes, most everything was cleared up. I do have a question and a favor to ask."

"Anything for you. Fire away."

"First, I'd like to know why you said Nick had fucked up?"

"When did I say that, sweetheart?"

"On the island, after my…um…my blow-up, when we were talking in the lobby. You said 'Nick fucked up' and you said you couldn't deny it. What were you talking about if the whole situation with Cynthia was a misunderstanding?"

"OH! Now I remember. I didn't say he fucked up. I said, 'he's fucked up' as in 'he IS fucked up.' As in...he makes questionable decisions."

"My God, could there BE any more misinterpretations!? Why would you say that?"

"It was clear from your, shall we call it, episode, that you were drawing conclusions based on some of his iffy decisions. You know how he can't separate from work, his work ends up becoming his life. And while I knew Cynthia was going to be on the show, *he* didn't want to tell you because he thought it would be fun for you to see first hand. Again, not a brilliant idea."

"OH MY GOD!" Anna started laughing so hard tears were falling from her eyes. "Sorry. I'm not sure why this tickled my funny bone. Probably because of the absurdity, and it's another misinterpretation on my part." Once she was half composed, she continued, "Thank you for clearing that up. Now I have a favor to ask. I feel horrible for doubting Nick and-"

"Sweetie, it wasn't so hard to see how you started connecting the dots, incorrectly, mind you, but I felt for you. I also knew, I mean know, Nick could never look at another woman. He's the only heterosexual man I know who doesn't want to go into a strip club for a bachelor party because he respects you so much."

"I know he does, and that is why I want to do something *big*. A grand gesture to let him know I'm sorry. I want him to know how much I love him and that *I* know how much he loves me."

"Okay, I can see that you two need some time together. What do you need from me?"

"I need you to get me on True Loves, without Nick finding out."

***

"You're going to do what?" Beth asked, almost choking on her drink. Lauren and Beth sat at Anna's kitchen island while Anna busied herself, putting charcuterie on a plate. Lauren patted Beth's back while she cleared her throat and caught her breath. It was Friday night, and the three friends decided to spend the evening in so Anna could update Beth.

"I'm going to be a contestant on True Loves," Anna repeated herself and added, "I'm going to ask Nick to forgive me for doubting his love and ask him to start a family."

Lauren took a sip of her drink and said to Beth, "I was just as shocked when she told me."

Beth's mouth hung open a moment before she said, "So, you, who didn't attend your college graduation because you didn't want to walk across a stage, are going to subject yourself to television cameras. This sounds very romantic, but what happens if you have a panic attack?" It was no secret that Anna's introverted nature lent her to panic attacks from intense situations.

"Gee, thanks for your vote of confidence. I've been working on my issues. And technically there isn't a stage at the filming. I'll just be sitting in a beach chair and talking directly to Nick. I'll have to ignore the cameras as best as I can." Anna pushed the plate of meats and cheeses between her two friends, telling them to eat. "This fiasco has got me thinking a lot about our marriage and what I want out of life. When I thought Nick was cheating on me, or worse falling out of love with me, I still loved him. I was blinded by the anger but still loved him and wanted him. I knew if he didn't want to be with me anymore, I'd have to let him go. I didn't admit it to him, but if it were just an affair, I think I'd have tried to work it out with him. I was willing to get to the bottom of it if it meant we could heal and continue to be together. THANK GOD it was neither, only my imagination gone wild!"

Lauren spoke through chewing a piece of prosciutto and asked, "Is anyone going to mention Anna wanting to start a family?" She swallowed to emphasize, "HELLO, that is huge news!"

"I'm still shocked she's going to go on a television show. But, yeah, Anna, where's that coming from?" Beth looked at Anna expectantly.

"I've been thinking about it for a while. Before we got married, Nick and I agreed we both want children. We just wanted to build our careers a bit. Well, I think it's safe to say we've built them. If we wait too much longer, I'll be a geriatric pregnant woman. Seriously, my gynecologist said that to me when we discussed it at my last visit."

"Oh, boy. That does not bode well for me. I'm not even close to married, and I'm almost two years older than you!" Lauren blurted out.

"It doesn't make it impossible, Lauren. The doctors will just have to watch us more closely than a younger mom. Tons of women have babies in their late thirties, even forties!" Anna realized what she said had been insensitive to her friends. "The point I was *trying* to make is there isn't a reason for us to wait any longer. One of us needs to be the impetus for a baby to happen. If neither of us says anything, we would just go on as we have been. And since he hasn't mentioned it, I will."

"You don't think throwing a baby into the mix isn't an attempt to fix what you think has been wrong?" Lauren is never one to shy away from a direct question, giving one or taking one.

"We want a family. I do, and he did. I guess I'll find out in Santorini if he still wants that with me. Nick and I love each other. Am I worried he won't be around because of work? Yes, at times, I worry that. I know his work will continue to keep him away, but I also know that I can handle him being away. We will have to work at making time for each other – taking real vacations, for instance – and that will make it easier during the times apart."

"It sounds like you have it all figured out, Anna," Beth smiled at her friend.

"I have nothing figured out. All I can do is have faith. Nick could cheat on me tomorrow, or I could, if I so chose. There is no perfect relationship. We need to work on our relationship, just like anyone else. The point is that I will choose to work on it. And when he forgets, I'll remind him."

"A lot of smug marrieds, as Bridget Jones would say,

make it look so frickin' easy," Lauren huffed.

"It can be," Anna said wistfully. "There are huge chunks of time when it's effortless. Just being there for each other. Enjoying each other's company. It's when the mundane sets in, work gets complicated, money becomes an issue, or an illness or family drama ensues. That is when the hard work is needed; not take each other for granted; be a rock for each other; show each other affection even when you want to pull away; be selfless and selfish at the same time; give one another what they need but also make sure you get what you need." Anna takes a sip of her drink. "I didn't speak to Nick when I started to have these feelings, and I let them build up. I should have been talking to him about starting a family when it was first on my mind, instead of putting it aside, on the back burner." Anna inhaled deeply and exhaled. "Next week is my chance. I'm willing to make a fool of myself to show him how serious I am."

Beth asked, "When are you heading back to Greece?"

"Steven wants me to be there no later than Wednesday because they will film the last episode on Thursday. They don't want to run into the following week, and he said so far filming has stayed on schedule. They've had a few late days but haven't had to shoot an episode in more than one day. That's the good news. I should be able to get this done in one day. My flight is on Monday. I wanted to give myself time to adjust to the time change. The only issue I see is that Nick and I have been talking every day, so I'll need to figure out how to be tied up for the 20-hour flight. He's usually busy for 10 or 12 hours, but if I don't answer or get back to him relatively quickly, he'll wonder or worry."

Lauren raised a finger like a light bulb went off in her head. "What about telling him you've gotten a cold bug, are taking the day out of work to nap and will call him when you wake?"

"That's not a bad idea. I'll text Nick just before I get on the flight, and by the time he reads it, he won't bother responding, afraid to wake me. He's courteous like that." She smiled smugly. "Looks like the plan is still in motion."

EIGHTEEN

When Anna landed in Greece, she checked her phone frantically. She had texted Nick at each layover then made up an excuse to be away from the phone- napping, eating, or bathing. Thankfully he had to go to bed, so Anna made it to Greece without further stress. Anna told him she would text him the next day. Now, it was the next day, and Anna was finally in Greece, in the same time zone as Nick, so she had to remember it was seven hours earlier in Santa Monica. Anna felt comfortable texting him a "good morning," even though it was the afternoon in Santorini. She texted she was feeling better and had a busy day at work to catch up on her missed day. Smiling to herself on the cab ride to her hotel, she tucked her phone back into her purse after he signed off.

Anna chose to stay at a hotel a short ride from the beach hotel where Nick was filming. She didn't want to take a chance that she would run into him. Steven had been adamant that Nick was staying at the beach hotel with the rest of the crew, and their schedule left them little time to go exploring save for the weekends. Steven also assured Anna that she was far enough from the filming location that she could enjoy the surrounding area without being recognized.

Anna checked herself into the small bed and breakfast she had reserved just a few days prior. From the front door of the quaint hotel, she had an uninterrupted view of Perissa's black sand beach. A stout older woman who barely reached Anna's shoulder showed Anna to her room and told Anna where to find the nearest restaurant. She decided to put on her swimsuit and walk down to the beach to enjoy the warmer weather that day. With a towel tucked under one arm and her tote bag on the other, she crossed the small road to the beach. Either direction she looked was black sand. She had noticed on her first trip the sand at the beach hotel was dark gray, but she hadn't known the volcanic sand could take on the shade of onyx. It was a notable contrast to the faded silver boards leading down the beach. At the end of the boardwalk, she slipped off her sandals and eased her toes into the black sand. If she closed her eyes, she couldn't feel any difference from the sand of the California beaches. The sand was fine-grained, almost like stepping into granulated sugar. The sensation made her instantly relax. She made her way over to an empty chaise under a straw umbrella. Looking around for anyone who might be able to tell her if the chairs were for rent, she heard her phone buzz in her bag.

She rummaged through her bag until her hand landed on her phone. She glimpsed Steven's name on the screen before swiping to answer.

"Hi, Steven! I'm here!" Anna whispered loudly and excitedly into the phone.

"Where are you, exactly, Anna?" Steven asked. His voice sounded strained in Anna's ear.

"On island, Steven. What's going on?" She didn't like that he used her name in case Nick was around.

"Anna, listen carefully. I'm not supposed to be telling you this. Nick swore me to secrecy, and you know I normally would never break a promise, but since you had me sworn to secrecy first, I owe you this. Aaaand, since I knew you were already on your way here, I know I should let you know..."

"Let me know what? What is going on? What did Nick tell you?"

"Anna, Nick is planning to fly home early. He wants to get home to you. I don't know what to do, I tried to tell him not to book a flight, that we need him here, but he insists I've got it covered and he needs to go home. You've got to do something before he gets on a flight back to L.A.!"

Anna dropped her bag and plopped on the chaise. "Steven, calm down, where is Nick?" Anna felt anything but calm as she directed Steven to do just that.

"We've just wrapped, and he has gone back up to his room, presumably to find a flight out for tomorrow." Steven sounded frantic. Anna could tell he was just as invested in this ruse as she was.

"Oh, God. He can't. I just got here. You've got to stop him."

"That's what I'm telling you – I've been trying to stall him, and he is firm that he will not spend another day away from you. It's quite romantic really, but stressing me out since I know you are here! Get over here, you can show up, and he'll be shocked."

"Or you could come to me. Tell Nick you'll take him out to dinner for his last night, and I'll be here."

"But that won't have stopped him from booking his flight. Are you sure you don't want to show up on his doorstep in a negligée?"

"I'm in a bikini right now, that'll have to do. I'm on my way. Text me the hotel address, please." Anna snatched her tote bag and sandals and briskly walked back up to her hotel. At the front desk, she asked for a cab as soon as possible. Within five minutes, Anna was seated in the back of the silver Mercedes cab and on her way to Nick's hotel.

***

"Nick, what's the rush? There are only a few more days of filming left." Steven was in Nick's room watching him pack.

"I only hosted the first few because Cynthia was nervous and wanted me there. After we handed hosting duties to *Ron Burgundy*," referencing the playful nickname for the regular show host, Brett, "I've been mainly hanging around to make sure things go smoothly. Now that we're down to the last couple, I have complete faith in you to handle it. I need to get back home." Nick paused after placing his toiletry bag in the suitcase, and looked up at Steven. "I felt terrible that I let Anna leave the island in the first place, and now she's gotten sick. I want to be there for her and let her know that she means more to me than work. I have to start prioritizing, and she is the top of the list. Work is a second, and it's not even close." Nick continued to roll his slacks and shirts into his suitcase. "I found a flight off the island tonight, and if I want to make it, I've got to go," Nick looked down at his Cartier watch, "now."

Steven was wringing his hands, trying to think of another way to stall Nick. "Did you say she was sick?"

"Yeah, just yesterday, she took a day out of work. She never takes a sick day, so it had to be bad." He paused, holding a shirt in his hands. "She was napping a lot and even said she had vomited. When I asked if she had a temp, she said no, that's why she could go back into work today." Nick threw the shirt down into the bag, forcefully. " Holy shit!"

"What?" Steven couldn't follow Nick's thinking and had no idea Anna had told Nick any of this.

Nick turned to Steven. "Anna's pregnant!"

Steven didn't know what to say. He didn't know if it were the truth or not. What Steven did know was he had to keep Nick from getting in a cab until Anna arrived. He was hoping it was any minute. "What? How? I mean, are you sure?"

"Didn't you hear me? In our line of work, we've both heard enough pregnancy stories to know those are signs, or symptoms, or both! I can't believe it! I bet she's waiting for me to get home to tell me. I've gotta go!" Nick zipped his case shut and rolled it out the door with Steven trailing behind. Nick stopped at the front desk to request a cab to the airport.

Steven quickly pulled out his phone and texted Anna.

911
Nick heading to airport NOW!
I'll try to keep him from getting in cab
Where R U?

Nick began rolling his suitcase through the lobby door to the outside patio, near the swimming pool. It was after five o'clock, and the sun was still high in the sky. Nick put his sunglasses on as he started to say goodbye to Steven. Again, Steven tried to convince him to stay, but he knew he didn't have a chance if Nick was intent on leaving. Nick began to walk away from the swimming pool, towards the front of the building just as he heard his name.

"Nick! Nick! Wait!" Anna had come around the building from the opposite side, the same way she had been led on the first day of filming. Coming into the courtyard she was standing at the side of the swimming pool, directly in the middle. She watched him continue to walk and knew she needed to get closer for him to hear her before he reached the cab. Anna looked at the length of the pool and knew she wouldn't reach him in time if she had to make her way around the pool. Kicking off her sandals, dropping her bag, and forgetting that she was still in her sarong, she jumped into the water and started to swim the width.

Just as she had started to jump, Nick turned around after hearing his name. He saw the splash in the pool, and when Anna surfaced, Nick's immediate reaction was to get to her. Nick ran to the edge of the water, pulled off his polo shirt and kicked off his shoes. Still in his khaki shorts he jumped in, meeting Anna in the middle.

NINETEEN

Anna had a huge smile on her face as he swam toward her. She had stopped swimming when she saw Nick dive in. When he reached her, he pulled Anna towards him, "What are you doing here? I thought you were home. Are you all right?" Nick peppered her with questions as he held her. One arm wrapped around her waist, he searched her face for signs of discomfort, running his other hand over her hair and cupping her cheek.

She nuzzled into his palm then took his hand in hers. "I was trying to surprise you until you got the notion to fly home. I had to blow my surprise to stop you."

"I am surprised! When we last spoke, you said you weren't feeling well and that you were in Santa Monica. Now I see you weren't home. What is going on?" He didn't give her a chance to answer. "Wait, I think I know. But why would you risk flying here to tell me?" Nick lowered his voice, "Flying this early wouldn't hurt the baby, would it?"

"Baby?" Anna scrunched her face, perplexed. "I wasn't sick. I was flying here and didn't want you to know. I'm sorry I lied to you, but I wanted to surprise you. What baby?"

"From what you told me...the vomiting, the fatigue, I thought you were pregnant." Nick's face fell. "So, you didn't have those symptoms?"

"I didn't." She then asked nervously, "Did you want me to?" hopeful and yet afraid to hear the answer.

Nick took a moment to look Anna in the eyes. He placed both hands on her hips, drawing her in close again, then wrapping his arms around her causing her breasts to meet his bare chest. Water droplets clung to his chest and biceps as he took a deep breath.

"Yes." Nick paused a moment and read Anna's face, her eyes staring into his asking to hear more. "I didn't know that's what I wanted until I thought it was a possibility. When I thought you were pregnant, I was excited at the idea of it. All I could think about was getting home to you. Even before I thought you were pregnant, I wanted to get home to you. I was disappointed in myself for letting you go that day. I don't ever want you to think anything is more important than you." He squeezed her tighter. "All the misconceptions because I didn't show you right then, in that moment, how much you mean to me. Steven can handle a few days here and there without me, and I'll do the same for him when he and Darron head to Hawaii. Which reminds me, I want to take you away. We both need a break. Work has been getting so intense. It's been 'get the biggest and best, higher ratings, outdo the other guy' for so long, that I forgot I still need to live my life. And you are the most significant part of it. You," Nick's mouth quirked into a smile as he added, "and the baby we're going to make." He bent his head and kissed Anna on the neck, hugging her tighter. She hugged him back and nuzzled into him but couldn't stop her body from shivering. He felt her shivers and said, "Let's get you out of the water. Do you have a room somewhere because I just checked out of mine?"

Anna was elated. She couldn't believe Nick volunteered the answer she had flown all this way to hear. He wanted a baby. He was ready to start a family. Anna let out a laugh, relieving the tension that had built inside her, "I do. I'm about a five-minute drive away."

As they climbed the steps out of the shallow end, Nick took in his wife's bikini-clad body. Her dripping sarong was in her hand as she said, "We might need some dry clothes for the cab ride."

Steven had been watching them and grabbed a couple of towels from a poolside stand as they exited the pool. He handed one to Anna, one to Nick. She dried her hair and wrapped the towel around her as Steven said, "I'm glad you two finally connected. That was pretty exciting. I wasn't sure you'd make it in time, Anna. My next step was to tell him you were here. And Nick, I had to tell Anna you were planning to leave because I knew she was already here." Steven let out an exaggerated, "Phew! I am finally off the hook, on both accounts."

Nick turned to Anna. "Why *did* you decide to give me a surprise visit? You knew I'd be done filming the end of this week."

Anna ducked her head, looking up sheepishly. "I had arranged with Steven to be on your show."

Nick was taken aback. His eyes widened. "*You* were planning to be on True Loves?" His tone darkened, and he crossed his arms. "With *who*?"

"Here we go, again, jumping to conclusions. With YOU!" Anna unfolded his arms and placed them around her. "Let's go somewhere to get dry and warm, and I will tell you about it."

Nick couldn't argue with that, he was beginning to shiver, too. They used the lobby bathroom to change into clothes from Nick's suitcase. Anna borrowed one of Nick's button-down shirts and wore it as a dress. They balled up their wet clothes and stored them in Anna's tote for the ride to her room.

Back in Anna's room, Nick placed his suitcase next to the desk as Anna walked to her case, lying open on the luggage rack. She took out a cotton dress, underwear, and a bra. "I'm going to take a quick shower if that's okay with you. Do you want to choose a place to have dinner?"

Her room had double doors opening to a balcony with a view of the ocean. Nick walked to the balcony doors and looked out. "Not a bad place you found. Do you want to talk here or at dinner?"

"We can talk here." Anna walked to the bed and sat down. Nick joined her. "Okay, spill it. What was the impetus for your trip here?"

"I felt awful that I hurt you because you mean the world to me." Anna looked down at her hands, twisting her wedding rings with her fingers as she said, "I've been feeling lonely." She looked at Nick and went on before he could interject, "Which I know is absurd, but I've been missing you. I know we are both happy with our jobs-which keep us *very* busy-but we would keep missing out on alone time, and I started to feel isolated. Add to that, you were spending so much time with your new assistant producer, who is *gorgeous* by the way, and I started to imagine the worst; that you could be unfaithful."

Nick placed a hand over Anna's restless fingers. "I hope that's settled now. I love you, above all else." Nick placed a finger under Anna's chin to tilt her head toward him. "Including work. That's why I told Steven that I am going to build in more vacation time for us." He smiled, knowing what she was thinking, remembering his foolish decision to invite Cynthia to their dinner a few weeks back. "Just the two of us. So tell me how you planned to be on the show."

"I called Steven to arrange it. He was going to have you host the last episode so that you would have to introduce me. When you did, I was going to tell you this: 'I'm sorry. I jumped to conclusions. I have no excuse other than the fact that I am madly in love with you. I couldn't fathom the idea that work would get in the way of us having a life together, so my psyche interpreted your late nights working as an affair. I did a lot of thinking about why now I was feeling this way. You've always had a demanding schedule. And I realize it's because I've been thinking more about starting that family we talked about when we first decided to marry. The baby we said we'd have someday. I want that someday to be now. I'm not getting any younger, and I don't want to miss out on having a child because we continue to try to grow our careers bigger instead of making our family bigger. I love you, and I hope you will take this next step with me. If you've changed your mind about a family, then I guess we have some talking to do." Anna held up a finger to stop Nick from interrupting. "After what you said at the pool, I know you are ready, and I am so relieved. You saved me from having to try to get through all that in public."

"May I speak now?"

"Go ahead."

"Can I join you?" Nick eyed Anna playfully and started to unbutton his shirt.

"Join me?"

"In that shower, you wanted to take."

Anna laughed and nodded, "I guess so."

"We're going to have fun trying to make a baby. And if I'm nothing but a perfectionist, we'll have to keep trying until we get it right." He stood up and gestured towards the bathroom. "After you. Do you need help with that?" He eyed his button-down she still wore.

"I've got it. Thanks." Anna began to undo the buttons, deliberately taking her time. She walked up to Nick, letting her shirt hang open and put her hands on his trouser waistband, sliding her fingers along the inside. When her fingers reached the front, she unclasped his pants and slowly slid the zipper down, rubbing against his erection. She separated his trouser and felt the length of him. Nick let out an encouraging murmur as he leaned down to kiss her while feeling his way up her waist with one hand to cup her breast. The other hand traveled south between her legs, brushing against her smooth, warm skin. She hadn't had any underwear to put on after changing out of her wet swimsuit, giving him unencumbered access. His hand cupped her, and he slid a finger between her folds.

Their breath mingled as they kissed, sucking on each other's lips and nipping with their teeth. Nick kissed Anna's lips, then cheeks, down her throat, tasting the delicate area that dipped next to her clavicle. He bent down and took one nipple into his mouth while his fingers danced along her vulva, finding her clitoris. Nick pushed gently at her opening with one finger and found her wet. He slid his finger inside as he made his way down her belly with his mouth. He stopped kissing her for a moment as he used his free hand to guide her backward. Anna thought he was going to stop so they could make their way to the shower, but he backed her against the wall and knelt. Placing his hand behind her thigh, he guided her leg onto his shoulder. This gave him the access he wanted to pleasure her with his mouth. She reached for him. "Just relax and enjoy, babe," he whispered lovingly as he gave her open-mouthed kisses on her most sensitive part while his finger inside her gave a come-hither motion.

"Nick, We're not going to make it to the shower. I'm

going to come if you don't stop what you're doing." Anna whimpered as she clenched her inner muscles.

"Come for me, babe. I want to feel you come all over me." Nick pulled his finger out partially and slid it back in while he kissed and sucked her clitoris. She ground into him as the orgasm continued to build. As he quickened his pace, Anna felt an intense wave of release, a moan escaping her lips. Her body went slack, and she slid her leg off of Nick's shoulder.

She pulled him up to her and pushed her tongue across his lips, parting them. The kiss deepened, then Anna pulled back, smiling, "Pay back's a bitch." She teased him with her hand. "How do you want to come? By my mouth or deep inside me?" She bent down and licked him.

Nick groaned, "It doesn't matter to me. I just want to hear you enjoying it." Anna took his hand and led him into the bathroom. She turned on the shower. As they waited for the water to warm, Nick kicked off his trousers. Anna turned to Nick and eyed him, appreciatively. He pulled her to him, kissing her while sliding her shirt down her arms and off. They stood completely naked, bodies pressed tightly, Nick's erection against her belly. She squirmed against him, eliciting another groan from him. "Not fair," he said against her mouth without breaking contact. Anna sucked his lip hard then moved down his body, leaving a trail of kisses along the way, stopping at his sensitive nipples, then moving farther south. She kissed along the path of hair directing her to his manhood.

She grasped his length in one hand and slicked her

tongue across the tip of him before slowly putting him inside her mouth. She lightly tongued him, pulling off and letting her warm breath glide over him.

She continued to tease him with licks until he growled, "I'm going to flip you over and show you the same treatment."

She put him deep inside her mouth and hummed an "Oh, yeah?" Nick fisted some of her hair, guiding her gently, making love to her mouth. He pulled back, hauled her to her feet, and lifted her onto the counter. Anna spread her legs in anticipation. Nick helped her scoot her bottom forward so he could enter her. He gave special attention to her breasts, sucking one nipple while rubbing his thumb over the other. Nick replaced his mouth with his other hand and continued to touch, pinch, and rub her nipples while kissing her deeply. His tongue danced against hers, then he moved to her neck, sucking while he pumped into Anna. Again, they didn't make it into the shower as Nick exploded into her as she squeezed his length with another mind-numbing release. They leaned their heads together. "Let's take that shower before we miss dinner entirely." Nick withdrew, kissed her lightly, and helped her down from the counter. They looked at each other, and Anna wondered if he was thinking the same thing; they hadn't used a condom.

"I guess the baby-making has commenced," Anna said with a laugh.

Nick raised his eyebrows, "I thought I made that clear. Did I not try *hard* enough?" He wrapped his arms around her and nuzzled her neck.

"I think we did just fine," Anna hugged him back, "Let's take a shower, for real this time." They both chuckled as they walked into the double-sized shower stall.

TWENTY

"**S**hould we ask Steven if he wants to join us for dinner? I hate to think he's on his own tonight because I'm here." Anna knew Steven and Nick would usually hang out or go to dinner after an episode wrapped. Anna finished getting ready for dinner and entered the bedroom area where Nick was waiting, fully clothed, on the bed.

"It's not like he can't handle himself. He does get along with the crew. But, yes, we can see if he wants to be our third wheel." Nick sent a quick text inquiring if Steven had eaten yet. It was typical for restaurants to open for dinner after seven, and here it was almost seven-thirty.

"Steven said he just sat down, and we should join him. We should hurry." Nick looked up from his phone, seeing Anna fully dressed and hair coifed for an evening out. "I'll call for a cab."

They headed to the lobby to wait for the cab. Steven and most of the crew were having dinner in Kamari, the next town over. Within fifteen minutes, they arrived at Taverna Dionysus, named after the god of wine. Anna couldn't recall if the name was the Greek or Roman God, but she liked the idea of it regardless. The tavern had a casual atmosphere, yet there were white linens on the tables with glassware and table settings. Anna and Nick walked through the bar to the outdoor seating area where more linen-covered tables were set up. Steven and the crew were at a cluster of tables that had been pushed together to accommodate a group. Steven sat at the head of one end and gestured for Nick and Anna to take the two seats on either side of him.

Anna was introduced to the six men and two women who worked for the show. A salt and pepper-haired man named Stanley, she recognized as the cameraman. She felt herself blushing at the memory of her erratic behavior a few weeks back that this older gentleman had witnessed and recorded. She was thankful Nick was able to have her part edited out. She greeted each one by name and realized they all had probably seen the catastrophe. She tried to remain composed, but her hands started to shake, so she put them in her lap. How she ever thought she would be able to go on a television show was beyond her. She was again thankful Nick interfered with her initial plans.

Anna took a sip of water to calm down. The worst was behind her now. She only had to recall their love-making earlier in the hotel to know that she and Nick were on solid footing. The memory of it heated her skin so she drank more water, as the waiter appeared and asked them if they would like something else to drink. She looked at Nick for guidance. He tended to know what she would like off of a drink menu regardless of the country. He ordered two bottles of white and two bottles of red for entire the table.

Anna listened in as Nick and Steven discussed the next day's planned episode with the host, Brett. Nick explained to Anna how everyone called Brett 'Ron Burgundy' because of his impersonation of the character. After Brett showed off his impersonation for Anna and the table, Steven asked Nick and Anna what their plans were after Friday. Anna realized they hadn't even discussed what they would do after Friday's taping. Anna assumed she'd hang around while they taped the last episode, then she and Nick would fly home together. Nick answered Steven by mentioning he wanted to plan a vacation for the two of them. Anna told Nick she could start to look into that. Nick wanted to be done for the week and take Anna away before she had to return to work, which sounded marvelous to Anna. She started picturing them holed up in a resort somewhere. Greece was beautiful and they could simply extend their stay into the weekend. Anna's thoughts were interrupted by a commotion at the other end of the table.

"Oh, man, Nick and Anna, you've got to see this!" Kyle, the Production Coordinator, put his hand over his mouth as those around him peered at his phone. All eyes were suddenly on Nick and Anna. Kyle brought his phone over to show Nick. Nick didn't say anything for a full thirty seconds. Anna couldn't take it any longer. "Nick, what is it?"

Nick held the phone close to his chest and said, "I'm going to show you this, but you have to keep your cool. We will figure out what to do about it, just don't freak out."

"So clearly, it's something worth freaking out over." Anna willed herself not to react. "Okay, show me."

Nick handed the phone to Anna. Anna watched the screen flicker over what she couldn't tell. It looked like someone was trying to record something but forgot to focus the camera on the action and recorded the ground for a few seconds. Then the camera pulled up, and she could see herself in the pool and Nick jumping in. There had been a bystander who decided to video Nick and Anna's reunion. The video showed them leaving the pool and zoomed in on her bikini-clad body then zoomed back out to show Steven handing them towels. The video looped and began to play from the beginning. The video volume was soft. She wasn't sure if it was the quality of the video or if the phone's volume was turned down.

She took a deep breath. "I understand someone recorded us, what I don't understand is how is it on Kyle's phone? I'm not blaming you, Kyle, I just don't understand how it's already viral, so to speak." Anna started to feel warm and nauseated. Just when she thought she was spared a public performance, here it was for the world to see.

"If you look here," Kyle pointed under the video, "you can see they hash-tagged True Loves. So whoever took the original video knows about the show.

It's in my feed from my friend in New York who also works in television. My guess is something they follow posted in their feed."

Anna gnawed her lip. "Is it possible to get it taken down?"

"You can report it as inappropriate and since they zoomed in on your body that might work. Other than that, it's pretty harmless," Kyle offered. "It'll take about 24 hours for it to come down."

"Twenty-four hours! In that time, it'll continue to grow and possibly be posted on other social feeds."

Anna was becoming more animated, so Nick interrupted. "Let's take it one step at a time. First, we'll report it, then we'll check other social media sites for the hash-tag True Loves. It'll become old news."

"Although," Steven interjected, "It's not exactly bad publicity for the show." The entire table looked at Steven. "What? Truth be told, it's nothing more than Anna and Nick taking a swim. You can't hear the dialogue, so people will be intrigued to find out what it's all about."

"That's the problem." Nick didn't like where Steven was going with this. "If they are curious they won't just want to watch the show, they'll want to know what's going on with this particular couple – me and Anna. We're not going public. It's no one's business." Nick's tone was severe. He crossed his arms in an effort not to hit something.

The table began to murmur. Everyone seated at the table had seen Anna's outburst at the initial episode taping. The only individuals present who knew the truth were Anna, Nick, and Steven. To onlookers, and let's be clear, there were more people present that day than just the crew, it looked like she was an angry wife, accusing her husband of cheating. Even though he hadn't been cheating, they didn't know that. For all they knew, Nick and Cynthia were having an affair while working on the show. And then Cynthia looked up her old boyfriend to rekindle that romance. No harm done on her part as a single woman. But Nick would be the cheating bastard. Fodder for a soap opera.

And so it began, flagging the video as inappropriate on any sites they could find. It wasn't arduous following the hash-tag True Loves. Over the next two days, Nick and Steven finished filming the last episodes, while Anna spent her mornings jogging the beach then lounging by the ocean. She didn't dare set foot near the filming for fear of drawing attention. In the evenings, she would join the crew for dinner, then she and Nick would return to the hotel to continue their baby-making efforts, which was no hardship for either of them.

Nick informed her there were a lot of murmurs on the set when he returned. He chose to ignore them. What could he say? He didn't love the idea of people putting their noses in his business, but they didn't know anything. It was a two-minute clip of him and his wife in a pool. There was no incriminating audio or video of Anna's initial accusations. Or so he thought.

TWENTY-ONE

T he next punch came while they were at the airport waiting for their connecting flight to Los Angeles. After making their way to the designated gate, Steven called Darron, and Nick turned on his phone to check messages. He noticed a missed call and a text message from Kyle.

I'm on a layover, so you may not be able to reach me when you get this. I'll call you again when we're back in the states.

Odd, why not just wait until they're back on the West Coast, why leave the text? Nick thought. He listened to his voicemail, and things began to sink in.

Sorry to be the bearer of bad news. Not only are the clips still up, but now there is a video of the edited part from the show, the part with your wife freaking out. Sorry, boss. I don't know how that happened. I'm looking to see who had access.

FUCK. Nick opened the browser on his phone and typed the hash-tag True Loves. The original clip could be found on several sites, but now there was a new clip and he recognized the scenery of the set. He put in his earbuds before tapping the link. Things were getting worse. There was discernable audio on the video. The clip was no more than two minutes, and then it cut to the clip in the pool. Someone had taken the edited clip and linked it with the new one. A lot of people are tech-savvy enough to do such things, but how the camera work got out was the problem. Someone was going to lose his or her job.

Nick struggled whether to show Anna. She had gone to the ladies room to freshen up. He signaled to Steven to come over when he was done with his phone call. Steven ended his call seeing Nick's distraught face.

"What's up, Nick?" Steven was almost afraid to ask.

"Look at this." Nick showed Steven the video. Even without audio, it was devastating watching Anna fall to the ground and retreat from Nick like he was toxic. "I'm afraid for Anna to see this." He kept his eyes on the ladies room doorway.

"Nick, don't go down that road. She'll see it eventually."

"You're right. I can't protect her from everything. I wish I could." He spotted Anna leaving the restroom and walking into a clothing store. He decided he'd tell her before they had to board the flight. "I'll be back."

Nick made his way to the store where Anna was browsing handbags along the back wall. "Anything catch your fancy," he tried to sound nonchalant.

Anna continued picking up bags and placing them back as she said, "I always love to look and see what's new. They're all gorgeous, but I have similar styles. Always love a fun color, though, like this plum is fantastic for the fall." She looked at Nick as she displayed the deep purple clutch in her hand. When she noticed his tense expression, she put the leather purse back on the shelf. "What's wrong? Are you feeling okay?"

Nick looked around them to be sure no one was near to overhear. "I just got some disturbing news from Kyle. You know how I asked him to look into where his friend might have seen the post of...us?" He didn't wait for her to answer. "Well, not only is the post still not down, but the edited video from the first episode is out there now, too."

Anna squeezed her eyebrows together as if concentrating. "The edited video? You don't mean the part with my catastrophe you had cut?" He nodded. "Oh, *so* embarrassing. And now that's out there, too!" She whispered emphatically. "But how could someone get his or her hands on that? What was his name, Stanley, the cameraman, he'd have access and then who was in charge of editing? And *why* would someone put it out there?" She mumbled to herself, trying to make sense of it.

"We've got a bit of an inchoate team doing the editing. Whoever can help out, will. Different eyes must look at it to make sure it's seamless." Nick had already been thinking these same questions. "I'll compile a list with Steven, and we will get to the bottom of this." This was why Nick was good at his job. He could attack any situation logically. He might be seething underneath, but he would always dissect any problem into manageable pieces and take action. He was an affable guy until he was crossed. You didn't want to be on the receiving end of his wrath. He didn't like the idea of firing someone, but when there was blatant disregard for the team or the production, he did so without a second thought. And this time it was his personal life on the line.

Nick and Anna made their way back to the boarding gate to meet with Steven. Once they were seated on board, Nick shot a text to Kyle for input regarding the editing team. He knew he wouldn't get a response for another 10 hours, at the least, but wanted to get the ball rolling.

Anna, Nick, and Steven were in the same row in first class. All three had lie-flat seats, though Steven's was across the aisle. Anna took out a small notepad and pen. "Tell me who you think of so far, I'll take note of it."

Steven started, "Well, Nick, Cynthia and I were part of the editing team," ticking his fingers with each name he mentioned. "Kyle is always around. Stanley does the filming but turns it directly over to Kyle, who brings it to the editing department. For this portion, it was Athena and Luis, and as I said, us. That's two performing the edits and five eyes on it, with Kyle and Stanley having access but not in the editing process directly."

Anna wrote this all down. "Where are all these people now?"

"Let's see..." Steven continued, "Cynthia took time off to be with Mike. She left the island after the first week of filming. Athena is a local, so she only worked on what we edited while on the island, the rest of the team has gotten several flights out between yesterday and today. Luis and Kyle and the crew will all be back in the office this week to continue editing and getting the episodes ready for air."

"Hopefully, Kyle will have an answer from his NYC friend as to where the post was from. Perhaps we can track it to an account." Nick realized it would take time to follow that trail, but if they could find the original account, it might answer who initiated it and why.

"Nick, should we involve the police? I feel so violated." Anna crossed her arms, shrinking her body, and Nick leaned over to put his hand on her knee, wishing her could wrap an arm around her, but the business class "suite" separated them.

"We can call our attorney and see what avenues we have. We may not have much of a case. We knew the filming was taking place. It was edited out, but it technically belongs to the studio, not us. There's nothing obscene, just personal to us."

The flight attendants began safety checks drawing Anna, Nick, and Steven's attention to the preflight safety video. They prepared to get comfortable for takeoff, popping gum in for the inevitable pressure on their eardrums. Anna took deep breaths to try to find a Zen space in her mind. She could feel the panic in her chest rising as she thought about the world witnessing her outburst. Nick held her hand during the ascent and asked her questions about her friends and work to distract her. A few minutes after takeoff, a flight attendant offered them something to drink. They gratefully accepted various cocktails to calm their already frayed nerves.

Steven was scrolling on his phone. "I almost forgot to fill you in, Nick. We have a meeting scheduled next week with Lance and Gary. They were sent the first episode and wanted to give us some feedback."

"Remind me who they are." Anna recognized the names but couldn't recall their respective roles.

"Lance Peterson is the CEO of TriCom Studios, and Gary Lister is the President. It's not uncommon for them to touch base at the beginning of projects," Nick filled her in. "The most frustrating part of this business is watching the crew work hard to get filming completed only to have the big-wigs pull the rug out from under us if they decide to do so."

"That's awful," Anna sympathized. "What might be a reason they would shut you down?"

"Nature of the beast," Steven retorted, "At this stage, the show will air. But whether we get more than this one season will be determined by ratings."

"I'm learning a lot more on this trip than I ever knew about your business. I understand what your job is, but I didn't truly understand how little control you have in the end."

"Yup, the studio holds all of the power. Studio meaning the people who get paid the big bucks," Nick said in jest.

"Because your paychecks are so tiny," Anna laughed at the two men's faces. They looked at each other, and then Nick leaned over to Anna. "Okay, we'll keep our mouths shut."

Anna didn't know what the Studio executives were making, but she knew what Nick brought home per episode. He did well enough that their mortgage was paid in full. She felt like she made peanuts compared to him, and yet Anna knew she was still making more than the majority of Americans.

They tried to sleep and ended up watching movies most of the flight, anything to keep Anna's mind off of her humiliation. She thought it was bad enough when just a group on the island witnessed the debacle, but now to worry over thousands seeing it. She felt sick to her stomach. She was thankful for the entertainment distraction and the occasional nap.

When they arrived in Los Angeles, there was a car waiting to take them home, another perk of not having to worry about every penny. It was after ten o'clock, but felt like eight in the morning, when the car dropped them in their driveway. The outside lanterns were lit, and a few lights were on in the house.

"Thanks for remembering to set the timers for the lights," Anna said to Nick once they were alone in the driveway. They rolled their luggage into the back hallway, leaving it to be dealt with the next day.

Exhaustion settled in. Anna could see it in Nick's face, and he in hers. He took her tote off her shoulder, placing it on the console. He wrapped his arms around her, and she rested her cheek against his chest, inhaling the scent of his sweater and cologne, a mix of patchouli and spice. Without warning, her body convulsed, and a sob escaped her.

"Oh, baby. We'll take care of it. It's going to be okay," Nick reassured her. He believed they would get down to the bottom of the video leak. Unfortunately, the damage was done. He hoped Anna could put it in perspective. They were okay. It was going to be old news eventually, hopefully sooner rather than later.

He felt a bitter taste in his mouth when he thought about outsiders not only seeing, but commenting on a snippet of his life. He'd been careful not to read any commentary, and he made a point of telling Anna not to either. It would only cause more upset. Initially, Nick thought the waiting was the worst, but he welcomed the quiescence. It was gut-wrenching to hear new developments that weren't a resolution. As it were, they needed to put a call to their attorney to see what options they have. He would call Rick in the morning.

Richard Gomez has been Nick's personal estate attorney for over 5 years. Once Nick started making a significant amount of money, he wanted help ensuring it was correctly handled. Anna became acquainted with Rick within a week of their engagement, when they combined assets.

Contrary to well-meaning friends advice, and Rick's, Nick didn't want a pre-nuptial agreement. Anna was the one who insisted on it. They ended up drawing an agreement that they both felt was equitable if the marriage were to ever be dissolved. While Nick made a significant amount more than Anna, she made a good salary on her own. If they had children, they agreed Anna would be the one to take time off from her career, so stipulations were made to address that. Anna had told him at the time it made more sense to have the agreement in place even if they both believed the marriage would be forever. He loved her exacting nature.

Anna squeezed him and exhaled a shaky breath. "I wish I could stop thinking about it. I had hoped I'd be able to put all that behind us. I thought when we left the island I would leave that embarrassing outburst there. Now it's out for the world to see, circling the social media realms."

"I know it doesn't feel like it now, but we'll be able to laugh about this. We know the truth. It was a misunderstanding. Something we had to work out between us. It doesn't matter what anyone else says or thinks. I'll call Rick first thing." Nick kissed her forehead. "We'll find out what else we can do to try to take it down. I'm not sure how you'll reconcile this in your head, but know that it doesn't matter. Really, it doesn't." Nick wished he could take away her shame and disconcertion. "We are human, like the rest of the world. So we had a spat in public. A million people can identify with that." He hugged her tighter. "Let's head upstairs and get some much-needed rest." He leaned down and kissed the end of her nose. She tilted her head up, and their lips met.

The kiss lingered, neither wanting to break the physical contact. It felt good to just be in the moment. Nick waited for Anna to initiate the separation of lips and limbs. When she said, "Okay, let's go to bed," he slid his arms down her back and took one hand in his to lead her through the kitchen to the staircase. They climbed the stairs silently, holding hands. When they reached the master bedroom, they detached and went about getting ready for bed. Nick was in bed first and pulled back the covers on Anna's side so she could crawl under them. Anna slipped under the covers and brought them over her. She nuzzled next to Nick, her head on his shoulder, his arm encircling her. They lay like that until sleep overcame them.

TWENTY-TWO

They slept until almost nine o'clock on Sunday morning. Anna stirred first, turning over to see Nick still asleep. She quietly slipped out of the bed as not to disturb him. She felt a hundred times better than she had the night before. "I guess it's true, things always look better in the light of day," she thought to herself. She went about taking a shower and getting dressed.

When she came out of the master closet, Nick was getting ready to take a shower. "Morning," Anna greeted, approaching to kiss him. "I'll start breakfast and see you downstairs." He noticed right away she seemed in better spirits.

When Nick descended the stairs twenty minutes later, he smelled eggs and something sweet. He guessed cinnamon. "What's all this," he asked, seeing the counters cluttered with ingredients and utensils.

"I made scones. They're in the oven and should be done in 15 minutes. I just finished the scrambled eggs," she explained, scooping them onto a plate from the frying pan.

"It all smells delicious, thanks," he came up behind her to kiss her neck. Her hair was pulled into a messy topknot exposing her neckline. Wisps of hair tickled his nose as he planted a kiss below her ear. "I didn't realize how ravenous I was until I came into the kitchen," he said as he stepped out of Anna's way, allowing her to bring the plate of eggs to the table.

"Good. Let's eat these eggs while they're still warm, and we can have scones afterward. Will you bring the coffee over?"

Nick took out two mugs and filled them, adding enough creamer in one mug to turn the black coffee to caramel, the way his wife likes it. He gave her a devilish grin, "I wasn't talking about hunger for food, but I have a feeling you won't want the eggs to get cold."

She laughed at that, "You know me so well. Come eat." Nick joined her at the table, which she had already set. In under-thirty minutes she could accomplish a lot when she set her mind to it.

After breakfast, Nick made the call to Richard Gomez, their attorney. He left a message and apologized for calling on a Sunday. "Rick, it's Nick Whittaker. Anna and I need some advice and thought you could point us in the right direction. I don't want to disturb your Sunday, but you always said to call whenever. It's not an emergency. However, we'd like some peace of mind as soon as possible. Thanks." Nick turned to Anna, "Now we need to live our life until we hear back."

"Absolutely. I'm going to go for a jog. It's a beautiful day. Do you want to jog around the pier today? We can stop in to say hello to Beth." In June, Santa Monica weather was perfect for jogging, reaching only a high of seventy degrees on most days.

"Sure. Let me get changed and I'll run with you." When Nick returned, he wore wind pants and a tee-shirt. Anna had started her morning in leggings and an over-sized pullover. She grabbed water bottles for them, and then they headed out to Nick's car to drive downtown.

Bethany's boutique was located a few blocks from the boardwalk where Nick and Anna chose to jog. After a couple of miles, Anna and Nick headed off the boardwalk toward the high-end shopping mall that housed Très Chic. Bethany's shop carried classic pieces, much like French women's attire: lots of black, white, grey, and navy. She also stocked classic and ornate handbags and shoes. One could leave her store with a complete outfit. While her choice of designers varied, she preferred to carry American designers as long as the clothing was cohesive with her overall goal. She wanted anyone shopping her store to leave feeling "very stylish" - after the boutique name.

The door jingled as Nick pushed it open and stepped aside for Anna to enter. Beth called from the back of the store, "I'll be right with you."

"Geez, can't get any service around here," Anna teased. Nick wandered the edge of the store where scarves and pashminas were displayed among the handbags. He had only been in the shop twice since it opened two years ago, both times to get a gift for Anna with Beth's assistance. He was impressed with the selection for a store with such a small footprint. It was cozy, not cluttered. Everything was prominently displayed, making it easy for shoppers to find what they are looking for or give them new ideas. Complete outfits hung at the end of a rack so customers could visualize pieces together. The key to her success was that she keeps just a few items displayed and additional sizes in the back room, where everything can be folded onto shelving. It takes up less space in the storage area that way. Nick had never gone in the back, but Anna told him that the back area was as big as the front of the store. Anna and Lauren had helped Beth unpack merchandise during the weeks it took to get the store ready for opening. Anna was envious of Beth's eye for style, always knowing what to mix and match for an effortless look: heels with jeans, biker boots with a chiffon print dress, a tuxedo jacket with sneakers.

Beth came from the back room, "How can I – Oh, Nick! And Anna! What a nice surprise!" She leaned in to kiss Nick on each cheek, then hugged and kissed Anna. "What are you guys up to today?" Beth walked to the checkout counter and started folding some t-shirts she had unpacked from the back. Anna and Nick followed her.

"We decided to come down to the water for a jog and thought we'd stop in to say hello. Anything in the back you're waiting to put out?" Anna knew if Beth got a piece in that she thought was perfect for one of her friends, she would wait to put it out until they got a chance to see it. It was a sneaky way to make an extra sale because inevitably, Anna and Lauren would fall in love with it.

"I just got the most beautiful navy sweater. I think it would look amazing on you. Want to try it on? Pair it with these jeans. While the weather is warm, add some sequin sandals," Beth walked around, grabbing the items in Anna's size. Anna looked at Nick and shrugged, "What can I do, she makes me feel 'très chic'?" She laughed at herself, the store's name always a punch line.

Anna went behind a curtain to the makeshift changing room. Nick walked toward the front of the store, eyeing a cashmere sweater he thought Anna might like. While she changed her clothes, she spoke up, "Nick, want to tell Beth your hypothesis regarding her fleeing date a few weeks back? By the way, Beth, have you talked to Drew since that night?"

That date night seemed a lifetime ago, considering everything that has happened with Nick and Anna in the weeks since.

"Drew called me a few days later and asked me out again. He didn't mention the abrupt ending to our evening, so I didn't either. He picked me up last Thursday after I closed the shop. I left my car here, and Drew drove us to dinner. We both had work the next day, so we returned here for my car, and said goodbye." Beth lowered her voice, hoping Nick couldn't hear her. "It was a very nice goodbye." Anna poked her head around the curtain, smiling. "What kind of nice? Kissing, fondling, more?" Anna whispered.

"Kissing with a bit of fondling. It got heated quickly then he stopped it from going any further, saying he didn't want my store to be the first place we made love. Though I would have if he didn't.... I think." Beth giggled.

"Did he say 'make love' or are those your words?"

"I will blush if I repeat his words." Beth's fair skin turned a shade of rouge. Anna snort-laughed, which got Nick's attention.

Nick approached the changing area. "What's so funny over there?"

Changing the subject, Anna looked over at Nick. "Nick, tell Beth why you think Drew bolted that night I told you about."

"How could you possibly know?" Beth wanted to know.

"Easy. As I told Anna, and any sane man will agree with me, a heterosexual man who declines going up to a woman's apartment, that she initiates, must have the shits."

Beth burst out laughing. "Ew, no way!"

"That's what I said. But Nick does have a point." Anna ducked behind the curtain to continue changing.

"I don't know why it surprises you both or why it's so funny. Drew was courteous, not defiling your bathroom."

"Oh, poor Drew," Beth frowned, "He was probably sick to his stomach and held it rather than use my bathroom. I wouldn't have cared."

"But it would have ruined the mood. Would you want to do your business in his apartment?" Nick asked.

"God, no!" Beth's appalled reaction got a laugh out of Nick and Anna.

"See? He had to go home," Nick crossed his arms, "No man interested in turning a friendship into something more would risk that situation."

Anna pulled the curtain open to show off the outfit. She wiggled her hips and posed for Nick and Beth. "What do you think?"

"I'm not going to look at the tags because I can tell you love it all. It looks great." Turning to Beth, Nick added, "Will you ring it up?"

"Let me take the tags while you change." Beth grabbed a pair of scissors, cut the tags off, and carried them back to the register.

Anna closed the curtain to change back into her running clothes. "Beth, when are we going to get to meet Drew?" Anna had heard Drew's name for months, and now that he and Beth were dating, she was dying to meet him, hoping they could go out as a group on occasion.

"It's still so new, I'd like to wait a bit. Let Drew and I get comfortable before I expose him to your inquiries." She waggled a finger in Nick's direction. "And don't think you don't act like an overprotective brother every time one of us is dating someone new."

"What? Guys can be dicks. I should know. I am one."

Beth looked up from the cash register, questioningly.

"A guy. *Not* a dick." Nick clarified.

Anna placed the jeans and sweater on the counter. Beth wrapped them in tissue paper and put them in a paper bag with Très Chic written in black script across the side. They hugged and kissed goodbye with Beth promising to call Anna after she closed.

By the time Anna and Nick started to head home, it was nearing three o'clock. Anna's stomach rumbled, reminding her they hadn't eaten lunch. To appease her suddenly voracious appetite, they decided to have an early dinner. They stopped at the grocery store to pick up vegetables and fish, returned home to bathe, and prepare dinner together. The shower took longer than expected when Nick surprised Anna by joining her. As they toweled off, Nick mentioned they needed a bench in the shower for their sexcapades. He proceeded to search online for a teak one to add in the oversized walk-in.

They were relaxing in the living room when Beth called shortly after five-thirty. "Hey Beth, all closed up? Are you in your car?"

"Yeah, I didn't get a chance to tell you that Drew and I are meeting up tonight for dinner."

"Or maybe you didn't want to tell me for fear I'd find a reason to hang around." Anna teased her friend. "Seriously, I will wait patiently to meet him."

"Thanks. I'm running home to shower. Drew is supposed to pick me up at six-thirty which doesn't leave me much time."

"Then I'll let you go! Have fun!" Anna ended the call

and let out an, "Awww, I'm happy for her," interrupting Nick from his reading.

Nick looked up from his book. "How's Beth? As if we didn't just see her three hours ago."

"She's going out with Drew tonight." Anna scooted closer on the couch toward him. "Do you remember those days? Dating?"

"Ah, yes. Having to put on a show. So glad that's over."

"What do you mean, 'put on a show'? Are you telling me you weren't yourself?"

"Not that I wasn't myself, but I had to be my *best* self. Like you didn't put on a show?"

Anna thought about it. "I guess the primping, always wanting to look fuckable, is a bit of a show."

"Babe, you still always look fuckable."

"Even in my sweatpants?"

"Even in your sweatpants. Preferably out of them."

Nick's phone buzzed, interrupting their banter. The name Richard Gomez lit up the screen. Nick turned the phone so Anna could see, then answered. After giving Rick some details of their problem with the social media posting he asked Anna, "Can you do four o'clock tomorrow?"

"I'll make it work for this." Anna hadn't thought about their predicament the whole day and now the anxiety came back like an unexpected ocean wave in the face, leaving her gasping for air.

Nick responded to Rick, saying they would be there. He saw the anxiety creep into Anna's face and wanted to kill whoever was responsible for airing that footage.

TWENTY-THREE

Nick and Anna had driven separately to Rick's office building. They met in the lobby of the building and took the elevator to the 9th floor. When they exited the elevator, a young receptionist seated behind a tall counter greeted them. They gave their names and she directed them to a waiting area as she picked up her phone to call Rick. Anna's heels clicked on the shiny flooring as she and Nick made their way to two butterscotch-colored leather chairs. Anna placed her handbag on the small round table nestled between them. A long charcoal couch sat opposite a large glass rectangular coffee table housing a neat stack of magazines and potted greenery. A plush rug underfoot made the area feel cozy as opposed to the hard marble flooring and soaring ceilings.

Within two minutes, Rick came down the hall, greeted them, and escorted them back to his office. The large office had glass double doors and floor to ceiling glass windows overlooking Los Angeles. A large mahogany desk sat at one end with two arm-chairs juxtaposed across from it. The other end of the office had a round conference table surrounded by six chairs. The perky receptionist entered behind them, asking if anyone would like a beverage. After declining, they all sat around Rick's desk.

"I can't handle this issue but I know who can," Rick told them after the receptionist closed the doors.

"Rick, we appreciate any information you can give us. Who should we talk to?" Nick asked, holding his annoyance at bay.

"I'm referring you to the district attorney's office for this. Social media can be very tricky. Given some of the facts you briefly told me over the phone, I reached out to a few colleagues, and we all agree, your best route is the DA's office."

"Ok. So that's where we should head?" Anna asked.

"You don't have to go anywhere. They're in this building. I've already spoken with one of the attorneys who will consult with you today. He should be here shortly." Rick's phone buzzed. He picked it up, listened, and said, "Please bring him down. Thanks, Liz." He placed his phone on the receiver and said to Anna and Nick, "Perfect timing. He's here now."

They all stood as Liz knocked and opened the door. "Mr. Gomez, Mr. Williams from the DA's office is here." Liz stepped aside and let the man walk in. His mustard-colored tie popped against his white shirt, complementing the navy suit he wore.

Rick began introductions, "Nick, Anna, this is...."

"Mark," Anna spoke his name before Rick could.

"Oh, you know each other?"

"Yes," Mark spoke this time. "Hello, Anna. Good to see you again." He leaned in and kissed her on the cheek. He offered his hand to Nick, "Mark Williams. Anna's brother, Josh, and I are good friends."

"Nice to meet you. Anna mentioned that you moved to the area recently." Nick appeared to be measuring him up. Perhaps seeing how handsome Mark is and remembering that Anna had spent an afternoon with him was raising his hackles.

"Yes, new to the city, not to the law." Mark seemed privy to the dick-measuring contest that was about to ensue. He was the expert here, and they needed his help. Mark wasn't about to let Nick's apparent discomfort with his and Anna's friendship interfere with Mark doing his job.

Rick gestured to his conference table, interrupting the tense moment. "You're welcome to consult here. I'll be leaving shortly for another appointment."

"What would you prefer?" Mark asked Nick and Anna. "We could also go up to the office on the 12th floor. They have conference rooms there, as well."

"Let's head upstairs." Anna looked at Nick.

"Yeah, let's head up. Thanks, Rick. I'll keep you posted." Nick shook hands with Rick, Anna followed, shaking Rick's hand, then they walked with Mark up to the 12th floor.

The DA's office was clean and welcoming. Not as impressive as Rick's polished floors and brass-edged front desk, but it was still more modern than most of the older office buildings in the downtown area.

Mark brought them into a conference room and asked if they wanted anything to drink. This time Anna accepted, asking for water.

Nick declined again. His cool attitude towards Mark was not going to fly if they were going to work together. Anna wanted to tell Nick he had to get his jealousy under control. Wait, he was jealous, wasn't he? Anna almost laughed out loud. She could play this up, enjoying every minute, or she could let Nick know that Mark is dating Lauren. She forgot to mention it in all the craziness that they'd been dealing with.

Mark stepped out of the room to get water, and Anna used that time to fill Nick in on Mark and Lauren. She explained she had introduced them at dinner a few weeks back, and they hit it off. So Nick needed to relax. She told him Mark is a good guy.

When Mark returned, Nick's demeanor was warmer toward him as Mark took out a yellow legal pad and asked Nick to explain why they were seeking legal counsel.

"It started with a bystander posting video of Anna and me in a swimming pool. It was posted with the hashtag TrueLoves, the show I am co-producing. Then within a day, another video surfaced. It was video shot from the show and had been edited out of the episode, video of Anna and me. I guess you should see it to see why we are trying to get it taken down. It's personal." Nick picked up his phone to find the clip. It wasn't hard once he typed the hashtag True Loves into Instagram. As Nick pulled up the clip,

Mark wondered what exactly he was about to see. He wasn't sure if he could handle seeing Anna in a compromising position. Mark imagined seeing her naked and swallowed. If this were too delicate to handle, he'd have to pass it on to a colleague, but he wanted to take this case and help his friend's sister and her husband.

Mark exhaled relief when he saw the clip of fully clothed Anna and Nick. Nick turned up the volume so Mark could hear it was a lover's spat. Anna winced when the part of the video played of her falling on her bottom. The video linked to the amateur video of Nick and Anna in the pool. Anna in a bikini and Nick semi-clothed.

"There's no clear sound on the second part so I can see why it's trending. It's intriguing. Looks like you made up in this pool clip. And you say the hashtag is True Loves. Seems like some propaganda for the show. Unfortunately for them, it's being used without your consent. We need to find out where the post started to see if we have a case." Mark made some notes on his legal pad. "Both videos were taken in public. While you may feel this is an intrusion on your private life, you were in a public space when this happened, so you left yourselves open to this. However, if someone stands to make a profit off of your public display, then you have a case. If the party responsible for the post won't profit from it, then you'll have to consider if you want to sue for emotional harm. But I'm getting ahead of myself. The first step is to track down the source of the post." Mark waited a moment to let all he'd said sink in. "Shall we continue?"

Nick and Anna looked at each other. "What happens next?" Anna asked Mark.

Mark made more notes as he spoke. "Following the hashtag back as far as it goes to the date you mentioned."

Nick spoke up, "I asked a friend if he can start tracing where the post came from. Over forty-two thousand posts are using that hashtag, so it's a lot to weed through. Will your department handle that?"

"Yes. If you want to pursue this, we'll start the process." Mark looked at Anna and Nick for confirmation.

Anna twisted her hands in her lap, "I want it taken down. Do whatever it takes."

"Ok. I'll be in touch when we have news." Mark stood and extended his hand. Nick and Anna stood and shook it. "Thanks, Mark," Nick placed his hand on Anna's back as they left the conference room.

Once they were back outside, Nick stopped Anna. "What do you think of all this?"

"I'm frustrated. If there is no monetary gain for whoever posted it, then we have no recourse?"

"That's not completely true. Mark said there would be other avenues, but he wants to take it one step at a time. I agree with him. We have to find out where the post originated, and that might go a long way to finding out if we have any leeway in having it taken down." Nick kissed her on the cheek, and they made plans to meet at home for dinner together.

As Nick watched Anna drive away, he had a suspicion that nothing was going to come easy to resolve this. He tried to make sense of the hashtag True Loves. If someone involved with the show posted it to create hype, why wouldn't they have informed Nick about it? Why not ask for his permission?

***

The next morning Nick arrived at his office ready to work on the final edits of the remaining episodes. He also planned to follow up with Kyle and see if there were any leads as to where Kyle's friend saw the posting.

As he made his way to his office he saw Steven's door was open, so he poked his head in. "Good morning. How goes it?" He entered, watching Steven pour over papers, and sat in a chair across from him.

"Getting ready for our meeting upstairs," Steven replied.

"Shit. Is that today?" Nick looked over the paperwork on Steven's desk, picking up a stack of scripts, thinking it would make him look prepared.

"No, it's Wednesday. Do you ever look at your calendar?" Steven feigned annoyance.

"Yes, when I get into my office. But seeing how I came to say hello to you first... What are you preparing exactly?"

"When you read the email I sent, you'll see that we need to discuss the promotion of the True Loves and where things stand for the detective series pitch for late July." Steven and Nick hit the jackpot when Tri-Comm studios offered them an exclusive deal. They only pitch to TriComm and are assigned to work on

TriComm's projects.

"Ok. I'll grab my notes on the pitch. As far as promotion for True Loves, I wonder if they're privy to the latest trending post. We normally have a month before they announce a show to advertisers, but with this most recent fiasco, I think they might get picked up sooner. I can't believe inviting my wife to watch filming has turned into this."

"Nick, I think we both know why you invited her there."

Nick angled his head. He shouldn't be surprised Steven would sense the reason he asked Anna to the taping. Being friends and colleagues for almost ten years Steven seemed to know Nick better than Nick knew himself. "I knew she was getting jealous. She started voicing her concerns, and I wanted her to see there was nothing to worry about with Cynthia, since Cynthia was on the show to reconnect with Mike. I had no idea it would turn into this." Nick's eyes were downcast, as if ashamed for bringing his wife into his world of reality television. Now they were cast members without signing up for it. "Now that I know the meeting isn't until Wednesday, that gives me time to do some more digging. I'll see you at lunch." Nick left Steven's office and headed into his own next door.

First on his agenda was to contact Kyle and then head down to the editing department and speak with Luis. Maybe Luis would have an idea who swiped the edited content. Perhaps it was Luis.

TWENTY-FOUR

It hadn't taken Kyle very long to find the original post. He followed the hashtag to the days preceding the day he found it posted. He was surprised Nick didn't know about it.

"Hey Kyle, so what did you find?" Nick put the phone on speaker in his office.

"Nick, it's TriComm." Kyle's bluntness put Nick on edge.

"What's TriComm?"

"The original post. I traced the hashtag 'trueloves' back to the day before I saw the posting, and it's posted on TriComm's Instagram page. Weird, right?"

"Yeah, weird. Thanks. I'll touch base soon." Nick disconnected the call. Questions swam in his head. *Who had access to post on the TriComm Studios page? Why would they post without his consent? Were the studio heads aware of this?*

Nick walked out of his office and headed down the hall. He still wanted to speak with Luis to see if he could sort out who might've taken the edited video clip and uploaded it to social media. He made his way to the editing room, where Luis greeted him. "Hey, Nick, are you ready to review some episodes I've worked on?"

"Just about. I have a question for you," Nick continued, "Do you remember when we edited out the clip of my wife.... interrupting the show?"

"Yeah, of course."

"Do you know what happened to that clip? Was it deleted?" Nick knew it wasn't.

"Nah. Cynthia said she needed it. She said something about promotional material." Luis looked at Nick's face. "Did I do something wrong, Nick? I had no reason to question her. She's part of the team."

"No, Luis. You didn't do anything wrong. Just trying to figure out what happened. You know it was personal and not part of the show. Now it's trending, and it's a little embarrassing, to say the least." Nick shrugged his shoulders. "I'll talk to Cynthia later. Let me take a look at that episode you edited."

Nick tried to focus on viewing the episode, but he couldn't stop thinking about why Cynthia would take the cut clip. "Let me come back to this. I want to tie up some loose ends. I'll be back later. Thanks, Luis." Nick left Luis in a hurry to contact Cynthia.

Knowing that Cynthia was on a planned vacation, Nick wasn't sure if she would return his message. He also didn't want to put her on the defensive by being accusatory, so he left a nonchalant message to have her check-in when she got a moment and that he hoped she was having a good time. Though in reality, he wanted her to get a sunburn.

By Wednesday, he still hadn't heard from Cynthia, and it was time for his meeting with the TriComm president, Gary Lister, and CEO, Lance Peterson. Nick tucked a pen in his pocket and carried his materials to Steven's door. "Ready?"

"Just a sec." Steven finished typing, hit send, and locked his computer as he pushed away from his desk. He grabbed his leather-bound notebook and a pen. "Let's go."

While they sat in the conference room two floors above, Nick fidgeted with his pen. It wasn't unusual to have meetings with the studio heads, but Nick felt anxious knowing someone had posted for the Tri-Comm studio's social media page. He wondered if he should broach the subject with Gary and Lance.

Gary Lister, president of TriComm Studios, entered the conference room first. His brown hair was tinged with silver at the temples, and he wore metal-framed glasses. He was in his early fifties and had been vice president before taking on the role of president five years prior when his predecessor retired. The gangly man walked in ahead of robust CEO Lance Peterson. Lance was of average height and build, with a burgeoning belly that was starting to pop out of his three-button suit jacket. He had a full head of white hair for a man in his mid-sixties. Nick and Steven stood as the gentleman greeted them both, taking seats across from them at the head and side of the table.

"Please sit," Lance directed. "This should be a

short meeting. As we told Steven when setting up this meeting, we saw the first unedited episode. It was explained that the portion with your wife would be edited out. First thing, we need Nick to sign some paperwork." Lance motioned to Gary to produce said documents.

Gary explained, "These are consent forms for the dissemination of the video clip you and your wife are in."

"Excuse my ignorance. I don't understand why you would want to use the video clip. And to my knowledge, it has already been disseminated." Nick played with his pen, keeping his hands busy.

"Nick, when the clip was brought to our attention, we had to agree this is wonderful press for the show." Lance paused then went on, "The network has already greenlit 13 episodes, but to get another season and at the very least make back the deficit that we've spent on the show we need some guarantees. Good publicity is one of the best ways to get viewers. More viewers mean more advertisers. You know how this business works. Hype! It's all about hype!" Lance's excitement was palpable. "So go ahead, bring home the paperwork to your lovely wife, or did you want to have her come in to sign?"

"I'll talk to her about it." Nick's staid demeanor did not go unnoticed.

"Do you have reservations about signing?" Gary asked.

Steven had been silent until now. "If I may, Nick?" Nick nodded. "I have witnessed how upsetting this has been for Nick and his wife. I'm not sure she'll be keen on continuing this type of publicity."

"Well, you and Nick will have to explain the benefits to her. Surely you can see how the success of the show will benefit both of your families." Lance had a huge smile on his face, looking at Nick, Steven, and back again. Nick felt sick, looking at this fat man who was greedy for Nick's private life to be displayed to the public. Nick swallowed the words bubbling up his throat, ready to have him quit.

"I'll talk to Anna." Nick clapped his hands, ready to continue the meeting when a thought popped into his mind. "Who brought this to your attention?"

"What's that, Nick?" Gary continued to move papers around.

Addressing Lance, Nick repeated, "Who brought it to your attention? You said 'when it was brought to your attention, you thought it was a good idea'. Whose idea was it?"

Lance looked at Gary. "Well, it was an idea that was born out of nonchalance. We had asked Cynthia for the first episode with the unedited video, and in passing, she mentioned what great fodder the footage was. After seeing it ourselves, we agreed. The tabloids will eat it up. The public will be dying to know what happens to this couple. Very exciting." Gary spoke as if he weren't talking about throwing Nick and Anna to the wolves.

"Even if we consent to you using us to promote the show, don't you think the viewers will be let down when we aren't a couple on the show? And how will you reconcile that I'm hosting the first couple of episodes and not a contestant? I think you'll end up pissing people off."

"That's step two. First, we need you and Anna to consent to using the video footage." Gary pointed to the paperwork sitting in front of Nick. "And I do apologize that it has already started blowing up, mixed signals and all. We had hoped to have this meeting before the footage was released."

"And step two?"

"We want to have you and Anna on an episode."

"But filming is already finished. It would be cost-prohibitive to bring everyone out again to Greece to film one episode."

"We'll film in the studio." Lance answered. "No need for the added expense."

Nick was flabbergasted. He had no idea what to say. "I need to talk to Anna about all this. It's a lot to think about."

"Of course. Let us know. Do you think you could have an answer by Monday? Time *is* money." Lance deadpanned.

Most days, Nick enjoyed his work. Today was not one of them. "I'll try my best."

***

Anna's day was productive, and she was looking forward to lunch with Lauren. They hadn't had much time to catch up. Her first few days back in the office were swamped, and now she finally felt like she was making progress.

"Ready?" Lauren poked her head inside Anna's office doorway.

"Yes!" Anna locked her computer screen, swiveled her chair away from her desk, and grabbed her handbag from the bottom desk drawer. Lauren insisted they lunch at the trendy organic Urth Caffé she was dying to try. They climbed into Lauren's black Range Rover and slowly made their way to the restaurant.

Anna was struck by the charm of the stucco building with beautiful tile work along the entrance walkway. Wrought-iron tables and chairs lined the front of the building, and yellow buttercups filled a swatch of green grass that framed the seating area. Lauren commented on the sea-glass colored windows on either side of the double doors leading to the café bar. The travertine floor accented the cherry wood and marble counter, giving an earthy, yet contemporary feel to the café.

An attractive older man with dark hair speckled with gray and a mustache welcomed them as they stepped up to the counter. After reviewing the menu board, Anna ordered a cheese and tomato sandwich, Lauren ordered a turkey burger. They both ordered organic tea and walked back outside to enjoy the sunshine. Santa Monica weather was perfectly temperate in early summer. Main Street was busy with people coming and going and the seating area was crowded with lunchtime business. They sipped their iced tea and people-watched for a few minutes. Anna noticed several tables were filled with couples in casual attire. She assumed they were tourists on vacation having the luxury of meandering over a cup of tea or coffee mid-day wearing sundresses, flip-flops, t-shirts and jeans. Bringing her attention back to Lauren, whose gaze was scanning the crowd, she began, "You're never going to believe who will be working on our case."

Lauren was aware that Anna and Nick went to see an attorney about the social media posting they want taken down. "Not Rick Gomez?" she asked.   Anna shook her head, taking another sip. "Who then?"

"Mark."

"*Mark*.... last name, please. That is a ubiquitous name."

Anna waited a beat and just looked at Lauren.

"*My* Mark?" Lauren guessed correctly.

"I didn't know he was *yours*, but yes. Mark Williams. He works for the DA's office, and that's whom we need for this type of situation."

"Can you fill me in on what's happening? I saw the video. I'm so sorry you're going through this. Have there been any repercussions? For you or Nick?"

"As far as I know, nothing detrimental to our careers. We went to see Rick Monday afternoon, and he referred us to the DA's office, Mark specifically. Rick is our estate and financial guy, so he doesn't handle this type of case. Thankfully he knew exactly where to send us. Mark is looking into tracking where the original post came from. He says our case to have it removed will be somewhat dependent on the motive of the person posting it. In short, if they will profit from it, we have a case. If not, then he said we'd have to talk about emotional harm, or something like that, as an angle."

Anna and Lauren's sandwiches were placed in front of them. "Thank you." Anna waited until the server walked back inside. "Honestly, as the days go by and nothing is happening, I'm starting to feel foolish for making such a big deal about it. I don't love that it's out there, and I would like it to be taken down before something deleterious happens. I'm sure I can't even think of all the possible ways having it out there could come back to bite me in the butt. It's our personal life, and it is embarrassing behavior on my part. Something I would like to forget but can't as long as it continues to be out there and keeps getting spread." Anna took a bite of her sandwich. Tomato juice started to drip down her fingers, so she put the sandwich down and grabbed a napkin to sop it up.

"That's awful. Do you feel better having met with Mark?" Lauren asked before taking a bite of her burger.

Anna sipped her tea. "I do. It feels better to have an action plan. Mark seems to have a good idea of where to go depending on what information comes back. I am afraid to keep checking the hashtag to see how much it's grown or if it keeps showing up in the recent tags."

"I'd like to know who started it. Whoever it was must have known about the show." Lauren took another bite of her burger. "This is delicious. How's your sandwich?"

"Messy, but good," Anna started to pick her sandwich up, then added, "Anyone present that day knew the show was filming. So the hashtag isn't a reach, but whether it was just some bystander or someone with something to gain is what we need to find out." Anna took a bite, chewing she waggled her pinky finger at Lauren. "Enough about this. Tell me about you and Mark. Weren't you supposed to do something together this past weekend?"

"We did. And we did not talk about you. The last thing we want to talk about is work after a long week. Anyway, Mark took me to see the Lakers/Cavs game Saturday night."

"Ooh, fun! Was it a good game? Watching live can be so thrilling. Where were your seats?"

"Lakers won. It was exciting to see LeBron play against his old team." Lauren was referring to the fact that LeBron James previously played for the Cleveland Cavaliers and is now an LA Laker. Anna was familiar with this tidbit as Nick was a big sports fan, and she'd heard him mention this. "We weren't on the floor, if that's what you're asking. Those go for $3000 a ticket. We were up high, which was fine by me. You could feel the energy, regardless of where you sat. It was a lot of fun. Plus, I didn't have to dress up – I got to wear jeans and comfortable shoes!"

Anna laughed out loud, "The sign of a successful date – comfort level!"

"The sign of a successful date is that he took me to brunch on Sunday." Lauren smiled smugly.

"Did you sleep with him after the game?!" Anna almost choked on her bread.

"No! We kissed goodnight, and he met me for

brunch the next morning. Then we had sex."

This time Anna did choke. Lauren clapped Anna's back while Anna coughed. "Don't do that to me!"

"It's all about the element of surprise. Mark would have expected me to invite him up on Saturday night. He wasn't expecting me to jump him after a Sunday brunch."

"But…where? How?"

"We met down by the pier to go to Mel's diner for brunch. Afterward, we went for a walk and ended up not far from Mark's bungalow. I asked him to show it to me. The bungalow that is. Then he ended up showing me more." Lauren laughed, cracking herself up.

"You're incorrigible! I hope Mark knows what he's getting himself into."

"Oh, he knows. And I am pretty sure he likes it." Lauren continued to eat her burger as if they were talking about the stock market.

Anna was happy for Lauren and Mark. They were both genuine people who deserved each other. "When will we double-date?"

"Whenever you want."

"Oh, I wonder if that'll be allowed?"

"What do you mean?"

"Mark is our attorney for now. We should wait until this is over. We can plan something the minute he's not 'working' for us."

"Ok. I guess I'll just keep him to myself for now." Lauren feigned wiping her brow as if it was a hardship.

They finished lunch and headed back to the office. Four hours later, Anna rubbed her eyes from staring at the computer screen. She checked in one last time to see if anyone needed anything urgent, then packed up her things to head home.

***

Nick stood in the kitchen with a bottle of Sambuca on the marble island. He placed ice in two glasses and poured two jiggers worth in each class. He eyed the clock above the stove: six ten. Anna had called him when she left the office almost thirty-five minutes ago.

A car's engine could be heard through the open kitchen windows. She was home. He took a deep breath waiting for her to come in the door. He listened as the keypad chimed and the door opened, then closed. "Hey, I'm in the kitchen," he called out to Anna.

"Oh, good. I'm starving. Did you start dinner?" Anna removed her shoes and placed them in the hall closet. She hung her coat and entered the kitchen.

"Yeah, I've got chili warming on the stove." Nick kissed her as she approached and handed her a glass.

"Thank you. What's this?" She sniffed the contents. "Oooh, my favorite." She took a sip. "But why? Long day?"

"You could say that. I was able to cut out early. Hence dinner prepared, but yeah, a draining day."

"Want to talk about it?" Anna took bowls out of the cabinet and utensils from a drawer.

"I will talk to you about it. Let's eat first." Nick took the French bread he had warming out of the oven and began to slice it.

"How was your day?" he asked Anna, shooing her away from the island. "Go sit down. I've got this."

"Well, this is nice. But I thought you had the hard day, maybe you should sit, and I'll slice."

"No, keeping busy is better. So you had a good day?"

"It was a productive one. I'm finally caught up, and I got to have lunch with Lauren instead of eating at my desk like I've been doing for the past two days. We went to that new organic tea and coffee house on Main Street. Urth Caffe. It was delicious. And Lauren filled me in on her and Mark. I thought it'd be nice to have them over for drinks, but I suppose we shouldn't socialize until we no longer need him professionally, right?"

"I hadn't thought about it. I guess so. It's probably better not to mix business and personal. So what did Lauren tell you?" He filled the bowls with chili and carried them to the table where Anna waited.

"Let me get some water for us," Anna walked to the refrigerator and filled two water glasses. Speaking over her shoulder, she told him, "They went to the Lakers game and hit it off. I should say 'again' since I saw they had hit it off when they first met. I might even say they're officially dating." Anna decided to keep to herself the fact that Lauren and Mark had slept together.

Nick brought the bread to the table and sat down next to Anna. She knew Nick would talk to her when he was ready so she didn't push him for more about his tough day. They chatted about some news articles highlighting the president firing more of his staff and finished their meal. Nick cleared the dishes, and Anna helped wipe down the counters. "I'm going to change, then we'll talk?"

"Yeah," Nick filled his water glass again, even though he wanted another strong drink to ease his nerves. He didn't like the idea of having to explain that the studio he worked for was the reason her indiscretion was splashed across social media sites. Worse, tabloids were now picking up on it as the advertising of new shows has started. The Internet was rife with suggestions of what was happening between Nick and Anna. At this point, no one knew precisely who they were, but it wouldn't be long before the publicity for 'True Loves' would show Nick's name as a co-producer, and his face would appear as the host.

Anna came back downstairs wearing an over-sized sweatshirt and leggings. She picked up her water glass and took a long drink. "Where do you want to talk?"

"How about here," he gestured to the sitting area off of the kitchen. Anna tucked one foot under her as she sat in one over-stuffed armchair, and Nick sat in the other perpendicular to Anna.

"There's no easy way to say this, so I'm just going to put it out there." Breathing through his nose, Nick hunched over his water glass, staring into the clear liquid. After a moment he looked Anna in the eyes and said, "The leak of the video was done by TriComm Studios."

Anna's eyes widened. "But *why*? Was it purely for promoting the show?" Anna kept her hands wrapped around her water glass, rubbing her thumb in circles along the tumbler. Nick picked up on the sign of her agitation.

"Yes. In a nutshell, the CEO and president saw the unedited version. When they were told it would be edited out, they came up with the idea that it would be a perfect promo for the show. They want us to sign consent forms."

"To what, *exactly,* are we consenting?" Anna leaned forward, placing her glass on the table and wrapped her arms around her upturned knee, hugging herself.

"For them to use our likeness to promote the show. There's a lot of legalese. I think we should have Mark look it over before we make a final decision. I'll send it to him in the morning."

"So if we give them consent to promote the show, will it eventually go away? Or is it available forever?"

"We'd be signing away our rights. To my understanding, they could use it whenever they saw fit." He paused to make sure she heard him then continued, "There's one more thing."

"*More?*" Anna let out an exasperated huff. "So, aside from us giving up any rights to having it taken down, what else could there possibly be?"

"If we agree to allow them to use it, they would also like us to be on the show."

"What!? I heard you, but *what!?* Why would they-" Anna flung her hands out letting them slap against her thighs. Frustration and befuddlement warred.

"Think about it...if they use our relationship as promotion for the show, how do they explain when that couple never appears on an episode? They need us to be on the show."

"Oh...my...god. *Where*? *When*? *How* would that work?" Anna could barely sit still, tucking and un-tucking her feet beneath her.

"They'll film us in a studio. They'll probably then splice it into one of the other episodes. It doesn't matter how. We have to decide if it's something we want to do." Nick watched her squirm and hated every minute.

"I...I don't know. I need to think about it." She dropped her head into her palms, massaging her temples. Nick bent his head lower to hear her mumble, "I'm already mortified... accusing you of adultery...to give up my rights to take it down...."

Nick's heart was in his gut, knowing he would be rubbing salt in her wounds. "It's already picked up by tabloid sites. It's already getting out of control. We need to decide quickly."

Anna looked up, her large brown eyes dull. "Can I sleep on it?"

"Of course, babe," Nick slowly stood up. "I'm going to get ready for bed. You wanna come up?"

"I'll be up shortly." Anna wanted to take a moment to think things over. She needed to weigh all her options. Nick bent down and planted a kiss on the top of her head. Before he could step away she asked, "Nick, what's the benefit of giving them consent and appearing on the show?"

"It would benefit the show." Nick sat on the edge of the armchair. "Hype for the show and then our story added to the show would, theoretically, increase viewers. And considering I am co-producing the show, financially we would benefit. The more successful the show, the more likely the network orders a second season. So by default, you will have financial benefit." He took one of her fidgeting hands in his. "But our personal life will be open to the public. A small part of our life, but nonetheless."

Anna looked down at their joined hands. "Do you feel one way or the other?"

Nick was hoping she wouldn't ask him this. He wanted her to decide freely. He didn't want her to appease him. Nick was willing to do whatever she wanted, but it had to be her choice.

"I don't. I'll do whatever you want." Nick kissed her, again, and left the room.

"Well, that's not helpful." Anna sat in the armchair and pondered the consequences of each decision.

TWENTY-FIVE

On Thursday morning, Nick finally heard back from Cynthia.

"Hey, Nick. I got your message to check in with you. How's everything going? I'll be back to work Monday. Any problems?"

The knot in Nick's stomach tightened as he spoke. He tried to keep his voice even and relaxed. "Hey, thanks for getting back to me." Nick cleared his throat. "Luis mentioned you asked him for the clip of Anna and me from episode one. Was that a directive from Peterson or Lister?"

"Yeah, Nick, from Lister. Why? Is there a problem? I sent them the entire first episode. I explained it was a rough copy and it would be edited. Are they pissed? I assumed the editing would-"

"Were you the one who posted it through the Tri-Comm Studios site?" Nick clenched his teeth together and felt his throat tighten. He loosened his tie thinking it would bring relief.

"I thought you knew I did." Nick wouldn't usually

cut her off like that. Cynthia was starting to sense all had not gone smoothly in her absence. "After Lister asked for the first episode he called me the next day and told me he wanted the edited clip to go viral. He implied that you were on board. At this point, you and Anna were on the outs. I was leaving for my vacation with Mike, as agreed."

"Why didn't you let me know? I thought we were a team?"

"We are a team. I just didn't cross paths with you again, and I took Lister's word that it was all on the up and up. What's happening? You didn't know?"

"No. Not at the time. Can you imagine having something personal like that splashed across the internet?"

"I'm sorry, Nick. I really didn't think to question Lister. He knew I was leaving and asked me to post it ASAP."

"Lister and Peterson brought me in yesterday, asking me to sign consent forms. I had a sneaking suspicion that someone from the show was involved…just hadn't put the pieces together that the studio would do that. Usually, it's the network that is interested in show promotion. I guess the studio wants to make sure they make their money back. So that's it? You were following Lister's orders?"

"Yes. Well…" Cynthia knew Lister and Peterson had salivated at her passing comment, "now that you mention it, I did say something that might have prompted it."

Nick was well aware about her comment but

wanted to hear her say it. "What's that?"

"I mentioned that the part of you and your wife was spicy. People would pay to see that. The next day I got the call that we would be using it as promotional material. I had no idea that they hadn't spoken with you. I'm so sorry. I made an assumption and was so busy getting ready to leave with Mike. I just pushed it through without taking the time to touch base. Again, I thought they had already spoken with you. Are you okay?"

Nick's gut instinct was that Cynthia wouldn't have masterminded such a scandal. He took her at her word. Lister and Peterson had admitted as much in the meeting yesterday. She had made a passing comment, and they ran with it. If only he could have been informed before his personal life was in the tabloids. Now he had to find out what Anna wanted to do. Do they try to make the best of the situation? Do they invite the world into their relationship? Allow the world to see it was a misunderstanding, and all is well? Will the viewers believe it? Does he care if they do or not?

"Thanks for giving me your side of it. I know you didn't mean any harm. Next time, let's make sure we touch base when an executive decision affects one of us. I'll do the same for you."

"I know you will, Nick. You helped me reconnect with Mike. I owe you."

"That was a team effort. Enjoy the rest of your vacation. See you Monday."

He disconnected the call and pulled his tie off,

tossing it on his desk. Cynthia's story confirmed what Lister and Peterson told him, but it didn't make it any easier to make a decision. He left it in Anna's hands. The business side of Nick would sign the contract in a heartbeat. It would be good business, a unique promotion for the show. The part of Nick who wants to keep Anna safe, tucked away in his back pocket where no one can touch her, wants to rip the contract up, and have the clip removed from social media. He clenched and flexed his fists. Anna had to decide if it was worth putting their life in the public eye. If she's okay with it, then he will be, too. But the second she says no, Lister and Peterson will have hell to pay.

***

Anna hadn't slept much the night before. Nick saw the shadows under her eyes and her pale face when she joined him downstairs that morning. They had coffee together before leaving for work and decided they would talk more that evening. If she chose to sign the papers, she would need to go into TriComm Studios on Monday. Nick told her if she needed more time to take it. He didn't want her to feel rushed. The studio executives would have to deal. They were asking a lot of Nick and Anna, and a few more days weren't going to make or break their promotional strategy. The truth was the longer they waited to decide, the more the clip would circulate. If they chose to be part of the promotion, then that wouldn't be a problem. If they decided to shut it down, it might make it more challenging to get it out of circulation.

Last night Anna had thought about the possible outcomes depending on how they chose to proceed. If they declined to be part of the promotion, they would need Mark and the DA's office to move forward, asking TriComm to take down the video clip. Then they would have to hope the excitement surrounding the clip eventually faded. If TriComm refused, they would have to talk to Mark about what options they had. Would they still have a headache with the clip in circulation? If TriComm removes the clip from their site, will Anna and Nick be able to get it taken down from other social media sites where it's been shared? Anna and Nick's faces are identifiable. Anna wouldn't want work associates or clients to ever see those videos! If colleagues have already seen it, should she go on the show to clarify and not leave people making assumptions about her marriage? What's worse? It's out there for the world to see or for people who know her to speculate?

If they choose to be part of the show's promotion, they will have to be on an episode explaining the clips and where they stand now. Does Anna want to reveal her relationship to the world? The people who chose to be on the show did so because they have a chance to be reunited with a long lost love. She and her husband had a misunderstanding. Why would that be of interest to viewers? Anna's gut was to say, 'No, thank you.' Why put her and Nick on stage for other people to judge their life. What would she and Nick get out of it?

By the time fatigue overcame her, she hadn't come

any closer to a decision. It took two cups of coffee for her eyes to fully open. After she and Nick parted ways, it took her an extra ten minutes to drive to work because she missed her turn. She chided herself for zoning out. Anna went directly to her desk without greeting anyone once she arrived. She didn't think she was going to be very productive today but knew she should stick it out, especially if she had to take time off next week to go to the TriComm Studio office.

Lauren poked her head in Anna's doorway a little before one o'clock. "Got a minute?"

After a third cup of coffee Anna's veins were full of caffeine. "Sure. Want to have lunch?"

"I was going to ask you that."

"Let me grab my wallet." Anna started to reach into her desk drawer.

Lauren walked in and closed the door behind her. "Before we head downstairs, I want to show you something." She came around to Anna's side of the desk, leaning a hip against the mahogany top. "Open your browser," she directed Anna.

"Do you want to tell me what this is about?" Anna said as she clicked on the Chrome browser icon.

"I know you said you've been steering clear of so-cial media posts of the 'Catastrophe of Santorini' and commentary, but I couldn't resist. I started reading the comments from the show clip, and you'd be sur-prised the feedback you're getting." Lauren logged-in to her social media account and searched for '#true-loves.'

Anna groaned, "I sound crazy. I don't want to hear

what god-awful things people have to say about me. This is exactly why I have Mark trying to take it down."

"People don't think you're crazy! They're on your side. They think you and Nick are adorable and are wishing you the best – just look!" Lauren pulled up the comments section and pointed them out to Anna.

So beautiful, love radiates from this couple. I hope to find a love like that.

This perfectly sums up how messy relationships can be. Love conquers all, but it's a road filled with hills and valleys, not a desert plain.

Did this guy really cheat on her? She has every reason to be pissed!

"It goes on and on with similar sentiments. Not one that I've read thinks you're crazy. They are rooting for you guys!"

Anna continued to read men and women commenting they hoped the couple would be on the show. They wanted to find out how it ended, and if this couple was still together. She sat in silence. Lauren didn't speak, allowing her to absorb the new information.

Anna let out a breath she hadn't realized she was holding in. "Well, I wasn't expecting that. I'm still not sure what I'm going to do, but I'm glad you showed it to me. Unfortunately, now I think I'll end up wasting too much time reading through comments for reassurance."

"Do you want me to leave you alone?" Lauren straightened from the desk as if to leave.

"No. Let's go eat. I'll do some more digging at home."

Anna grabbed her wallet, locked her computer, and walked out of her office with Lauren. When she didn't say anything on the walk to the elevator, Lauren said, "You're particularly pensive now. Are you sure you're up for lunch?"

"Yes, of course. It's just a lot to take in. I'm starting to see this whole situation in a different light after reading people's reactions."

"How so?" Lauren pushed the button for the elevator.

"I was embarrassed about the video going public worried how people would judge. I'm sure people are making hasty judgments, too, but knowing people are supportive makes me feel better somehow."

"Duh! Being judged by strangers sucks! Hearing that not everyone's a douche is relieving." Lauren could always make Anna laugh during tense times.

Anna softly chuckled and squeezed her friend's arm. "You always put everything into perspective. And say it so eloquently."

The doors slid open, and they walked onto the empty elevator. Lauren pressed the button for the ground floor to the café then stuck her tongue out before she said, "Just saying. This crazy world we live in is not black and white. I'd love it if all problems could be solved as simply as writing code. Put in a couple extra lines of words with underscores, and problems disappear. But there are all those lovely shades of charcoal and dove grey."

"Sometimes, I wish it were black and white. It would make this decision easier. I don't want to hurt Nick's career, but I'm afraid of leaving us vulnerable to public opinion. God, how did it get to this?"

Lauren shrugged her shoulders as the elevator doors opened. They headed across the lobby to the café. As they perused the menu board, Anna took several fortifying breaths and exhaled deeply, letting her worries float away on the air that left her. It was the best she could do for now. She couldn't wait to get home to run a hot bath and let the two cherubs sitting on her shoulders debate this decision.

TWENTY-SIX

On Friday, Anna conferenced into a phone call with Mark and Nick to discuss the paperwork. Mark confirmed TriComm had covered their bases, not leaving any room for Nick or Anna to sue them for any use of the video once they signed the consent forms. Mark was impressed, but not surprised, that the legal team for TriComm had ironclad consent forms. Studios couldn't afford to leave themselves open to litigation on something this standard. They were grateful to have Mark's expertise. Anna and Nick thanked him and let him know they would make a decision by Monday and get back to him.

***

"I've made a decision." Nick's heart skipped a beat when Anna's voice pierced the silence. Nick had busied himself with some scriptwriting while he had waited for Anna to return home. He had already phoned in a takeout order and planned to pick it up shortly. Nick hadn't realized how immersed he'd been in his work until her words broke his concentration. With a hand over his heart, he looked up from his desk. She stood in the doorway of his home office. "Hey, babe, make more noise when you come home. You almost gave me a heart attack."

"Sorry, you okay?" She stalked into the room on a mission.

"Yeah. I'll live. What did you decide?" He watched Anna pace from one side of the room to the other.

"Do you want a drink first?" She kept rubbing her hands together while she paced.

"That bad?"

"I'm not sure." She stopped and looked out the office window. "Maybe."

"If you're not sure, then give it more thought. There's no rush. Lister and Peterson can wait."

"No, no, I made a decision. I'm just not sure if you'll think it's good or bad." She turned away from the window and looked at Nick behind the desk.

"Lay it on me, babe." He leaned back in his chair.

Looking straight in his eyes, she said, "I'll sign the forms." He raised his eyebrows in surprise. "I mean, if you're okay with it," she added, twisting her wedding bands.

"I told you I'm fine with whatever you decide. We're in this together. So... are you one hundred percent sure? Once we sign, we can't go back." He sat forward, resting his elbows on his desk, his eyes following her as she paced the room again.

"No, but I'm eighty percent." She stopped pacing and flopped into the leather chair across from his desk. She ran her hands over the chenille throw that hung over the arm of the chair.

"And you're comfortable signing away your rights at eighty percent certainty? What's the twenty percent hesitation?"

Looking down at the lint balls she had created from her incessant rubbing of the throw, she stilled her hands, exhaled, and began, "The unknown, unforeseeable outcomes. I've mulled this over and kept asking myself, *what's the point of having us in the public eye*? We both know I'm not the most comfortable person with all eyes on me." She pushed her hair back, tucked it behind her ears and crossed her arms. "Lauren showed me the comments on the posts. I hadn't known that people could feel connected to strangers after seeing a short video clip. That people could find hope from seeing a blurb of our tumultuous relationship. I guess the romantic in me is willing to leave my comfort zone for that. So, yes, at eighty percent I'm comfortable signing the consent forms and being a part of the True Loves show." She expelled air audibly, ending her rant.

"Ok, then. Can you come into the office with me first thing Monday morning? Maybe you should take the morning off from work so we can discuss details with Lister and Peterson regarding a filming schedule. If you change your mind at any point, don't hesitate to speak up because once we sign, we're making a legal commitment. Okay?"

"Okay." As if psyching herself up, she repeated with more enthusiasm, "Okay!" And stood over his desk putting up her hand for Nick to give it a high-five.

Nick's palm met hers, and he laughed. The weight he'd been carrying on his shoulders felt lighter, witnessing her playful side and that she was going to have fun with it. "Cool, we're going to be on TV together." He came around his desk, wrapping his arms around her in a bear hug. "It's going to be fun. We'll work together for a day or two and then sit back and reap the rewards of a show well spun."

Anna attributed the tingle down her spine to nervous excitement. She hugged Nick tighter then leaned back to look him in the eye. "Do I get to go to wardrobe and makeup?" Nick angled his head with a quizzical look and one eyebrow raised. "What? I'm looking on the bright side."

"Of course you are." Nick's lips met Anna's, and she melted into the kiss.

TWENTY-SEVEN

On Monday morning, Anna woke before her alarm clock. She tried to close her eyes on Sunday evening and slept fitfully until six o'clock. Her excitement had exhausted her the night before. Anna watched Nick sleeping beside her, and her heart swelled. She eased out of bed, turned off her alarm as not to wake him, and headed into the bathroom to shower. As she lathered her hair, inhaling lavender and rosemary, she hummed a tune by Lewis Capaldi. She sang a few lines as she rinsed the suds. Her mind drifted to the weekend's events. She was elated, having finally decided to use the embarrassing video to tell their story. Nick assured her he was one hundred percent on board. When Anna continued to question him, he silenced her with his hands, mouth, and tongue. She finally relented that he was, in fact, happy to sign the contract.

Over the weekend, they had lunch with Lauren and Mark. Feeling confident of the decision to sign the paperwork on Monday, Anna asked them if they wanted to have a meal together. Bethany couldn't join as she had plans with Drew and still wasn't ready to share him, though Lauren had already met Drew on several occasions hanging out at Très Chic while Bethany worked. Anna was doing her best not to hound Beth about a group date. She was ecstatic that her two closest friends were in relationships that showed promise. How many times did one of them date a guy everyone else could see would not stick around, treated them badly, or the chemistry was severely lacking?

Anna ruminated on this for a moment. Before she met Nick, she had her fair share of disheartening relationships if that's what they could be called. Some of those *relationships* lasted a mere single date. One date barely lasted an entire meal. He kept insinuating that they should go back to his place. Considering Anna had not felt a spark, let alone a flicker, she excused herself from the table. Upon returning, she received a phone call liberating her from a torturous end to the evening. To this day, she is adamant that anyone in the early stages of dating have their own mode of transportation: car, subway, bus, taxi, uber, any means other than to rely on the suitor.

After her dating disasters and hearing her girlfriends lament finding the right guy, Anna beamed, knowing Mark was a perfect match for Lauren. Now she was dying to meet Drew to pass judgment on him!

The knock on the bathroom door distracted her from her thoughts. Nick slowly opened the door a crack so that Anna would hear him clearly. "Good morning. Are you taking the morning off to come into work with me?"

She called over the gushing water, "Yes. Let me finish up, and we can discuss today's schedule."

He blew her a kiss and closed the door. Anna finished getting ready and waited downstairs, eating oatmeal and sipping coffee while Nick showered and dressed.

When she heard Nick on the stairs, she said, "I made you some hardboiled eggs. There's juice in the fridge."

"Thanks," Nick walked straight to the refrigerator and took out the tomato juice. As he poured a glass, he asked, "Are you following me, or are we driving together? When do you need to be back to the office?"

"I'd like to be back after lunch. I messaged Sandy Friday night and told her that's when I'd be in the office," Anna said, referring to her boss. "I'll meet you at your office for the morning, then we can grab a quick bite before I head to work."

They finished breakfast and got into their separate cars. Nick rolled down his window and motioned for Anna to do the same. Once she did, he said, "For a couple of days, we'll be able to ride to work together." He waggled his eyebrows at her.

She laughed at his reference to work. It would hardly seem like work, getting glammed up and filming an episode. They had discussed that they would be paid for their appearance on the show. Typically contestants weren't paid cash. Instead, contestants received a free trip to Santorini, but with Nick and Anna filming in the studio, they would receive a stipend.

"Meet you in the parking garage?"

"Follow me. *I know all the great parking spaces. Believe me!*" Nick mocked the current US president's braggadocio.

Anna gave him a thumbs-up and closed the window.

The commute to Nick's office was close to an hour. Anna thought her 35-minute commute was long. She forgot how terrible traffic into downtown LA was on a Monday morning. Friday commutes always seemed more manageable, probably because Friday was the most requested day off. She knew Nick enjoyed using Audible to listen to books on his commute. She preferred music and the banter of radio DJs to entertain her as she sat in bumper-to-bumper traffic.

Nick waited for Anna to park then eased his car into the empty space adjacent to her car. Anna slid her light gray blazer over her pale blue silk blouse, grabbed her purse from her seat and locked the car. Nick walked up beside her. "Ready?"

"As I'll ever be," she linked her arm with his and let him lead her into the building.

***

The meeting with President Lister and CEO Peterson lasted just over an hour. Anna and Nick signed the consent forms, and plans for the finale were discussed. Unlike the other episodes, where love interests were revealed, the final event would be a question and answer panel. Nick would work with

Steven and the show host, Brett Taylor, to write the questions. Anna and Nick would practice their responses ahead of the taping. They would also invite the contestants from the first episode, who were present when Anna had cursed out Nick, to participate in the Q&A panel. They, too, would receive questions ahead of time.

Anna decided to head to work while Nick set a meeting with Steven and Brett to start working on questions. Anna mentioned a few comments she had read with Lauren that might be worth exploring to devise questions that appease viewer curiosity.

They had a few weeks to pull everything together before they would film. And yes, Anna would have a professional hair and makeup team to get her ready. She couldn't wait to share the news with Lauren.

The next weeks were relatively uneventful for Anna. As the question list was approved, Nick would bring it home so they could start composing their responses. The responses would accompany Nick each morning to his office to be authorized by the team. Then the process would repeat. Questions compiled and approved, answers formulated for approval until the team felt they had enough material to fill a one-hour time slot, roughly 10-minutes per couple. After several weeks the date was set to start filming. Anna requested the necessary time off from work and began to have stomach pains as the date approached.

***

"Dammit," Anna muttered. Carrying a glass of

water to the kitchen table, she popped two tums and chewed, plopping herself into a chair.

"What's wrong," Nick asked, scrolling through the newsfeed on his phone.

"My stomach's acting up again." She chased the tablets with the glass of water. "I swear, the closer we get to filming, the more my body betrays me."

"You think nerves?"

"Ya *think*?" Anna snarled at him. "Sorry." She propped her feet on a chair next to hers. "I just hate not feeling well. I keep imagining being on camera, in front of god knows how many people, and the anticipation is killing me. This reminds me of the time I was supposed to present in front of the entire student body in 8th grade. I hid in the bathroom, puking. When they finally found me and saw what a wreck I was, they decided to skip my part. I genuinely thought I'd be able to do it. But my nerves got the best of me. Similar to now."

"How did you ever get through college?" He asked, not really needing an answer. Any time she had to be in front of a crowd, they worked together to get her through it. She was never one to want a big elaborate wedding, partly because of her upbringing but mainly because she didn't want to be on display. They had a small intimate wedding with only their closest friends and family. It didn't matter to Nick, he would have gotten married at the courthouse.

"Not easily. I worked hard with counseling. It's just been so long since I had to do anything so public. As you know, I don't need to give big speeches or presentations for work. I am generally behind the scenes or dealing with clients at dinners out, not in auditoriums, or television studios."

"You need to chant your mantra," Nick joked. "I'm great, gosh darn it, and people like me," he butchered the old Saturday Night Live Stuart Smalley affirmation. "On a serious note, just look at Brett or me when you answer. Don't worry about anyone else in the studio."

"I know, you've told me. Will I be able to squeeze your hand? Or maybe I should keep something small in my palm." She laid her hands across her stomach.

"Absolutely. Both." Nick rubbed the back of her hands. "Sorry you're not feeling well. Anything I can do."

"I just need to take my mind off of it."

"I can help with that." Nick said looking at his phone's screen again.

"Be serious. I do *not* feel like doing *that* right now!"

Nick chuckled, smiling he told her, "While that is tempting, I was actually going to show you this funny sketch from The Late Show. Laughter is the best medicine."

Nick pulled up the video on his phone and angled the screen so they both could view it. They laughed at the antics of the show's host and celebrity guests, and soon Anna was feeling better.

Unfortunately, each day, her malaise returned.

TWENTY-EIGHT

Finally, the day of the show's taping arrived.

I think I'm going to be sick. Anna rushed to the bathroom and gagged. Once the nausea passed, she told herself, *I can do this. I've got to calm down.*

"Anna," Nick called from downstairs. When she didn't answer, he went up to see if she was ready to go. He found her sitting on the bathroom floor.

"Did you throw up?"

"No. Just gagging. I'm a mess."

"Hair and makeup will take care of it. Maybe you need a drink to calm your nerves."

"Nick, it's barely eight in the morning!"

"It's five o'clock somewhere." Nick helped her up. "Come downstairs, we have time for some breakfast. I don't think you should attempt this on an empty stomach."

Anna smoothed her blouse and slacks, grabbed her blazer and followed Nick downstairs.

Nick ate his own omelet while he watched Anna push hers around her plate. "Eat."

"I am."

"No, you're pretending to eat. I've watched you push those eggs from one side to the other for the last five minutes."

Anna scooped up the cheese-filled eggs and made a show of putting it in her mouth. "See," she mumbled around the eggs.

"Better. Eat it all. It's potentially a long day, you'll be glad you had a good breakfast."

"I thought they always had food services at studio tapings." She took another bite, suddenly ravenous.

"Yeah, they will. You never know exactly when we'll break, so it's better to be well-fed."

He watched her demolish the eggs and toast.

"I guess after not eating much from nerves, I'm finally ready to get some fuel."

Nick took his last sip of coffee. "Good. We should get going soon."

After clearing the dishes, they headed back upstairs. They brushed and flossed; not taking the chance breakfast could appear in their smile.

When they arrived at the studio, they were sent to hair and makeup. Anna watched in the mirror as they coiffed her long tresses and worked her face into a woman she barely recognized with sultry eyes and neutral lips. She couldn't remember the last time she wore so much makeup. Anna asked the artist about the heavy application and was reminded of the bright lights on set and how faces get washed out. When she met with Nick again, she saw he had an excessive layer of foundation as well.

They were led to the set, where the other three couples from the first show were already waiting. Anna's chest tightened as she recognized Cynthia among the group. She wasn't sure how Cynthia would act towards her, considering she accused the woman of having an affair with Nick. Nick squeezed Anna's hand as they approached the group.

"Anna, you remember Cynthia?" Nick reintroduced them.

"Hi, Cynthia." Anna held out her hand, and Cynthia shook it, introducing the tall, dark man by her side. "Anna, this is Mike."

Anna recognized him from the first morning in Santorini. "Hi, Mike. It's nice to see you again."

"Mike and I need to thank you, Anna." Anna tilted her head in question. "You are the reason Mike and I are back here." Cynthia lowered her voice. "After having an incredible time abroad now they are paying us to do this last episode." Raising her voice to normal, she continued, "It was hard enough going back to work after our vacation and now it'll be hard to go back to work after all this star treatment."

Anna smiled, exhaling. "I know what you mean. This is all very surreal for me."

Nick brushed her hand with his fingertips, "Let's meet the rest of the group."

A petite woman introduced herself as Callie. She held out one hand while she tucked a short, shiny lock of strawberry-blonde hair behind her ear. A smile played on her lips as her amber eyes moved from Anna to the gentleman next to her. "This is John,"

Callie said releasing Anna's hand and allowing John to grasp Anna in a firm handshake. Anna noted John's dark copper curls and deep brown eyes. Callie and John looked like they belonged together.

After greeting Callie and John, Anna turned to introduce herself to the last couple, Hattie and Saul. Anna could tell they were young by their smooth-skinned faces even while they wore huge smiles. Their happiness was contagious, Anna's smile grew wider as she watched Hattie's bright blue eyes look into Saul's as she smoothed his coal-colored hair. They primped each other while waiting for the next direction.

Nick addressed the group to find their seats on stage. Brett Taylor introduced himself as the host and they were taken through the show order. It was explained that they would work through one couple at a time answering several viewer questions. Nick, Steven, and Brett had collaborated with the social media manager to ask viewers to post any questions about the couples or show. They worked off of these and came up with a few of their own. The pairs had prepped their answers, and everything was typed into the teleprompter to keep everyone on track.

Anna had to admit she felt more at ease, knowing she had the prompter for reference if she started to freeze up. Nick hadn't told Anna that he had helped design the layout of the show, having everything written out ahead of time to minimize anxiety and prevent any impromptu inappropriate questions. They also chose to omit having a live audience as other shows have done. This final episode was about updating viewers. That was all. After this show, he and Anna could go back to a low-key life. Their 15-minutes of fame was coming to an end. *Thank God.*

Everyone was reminded that there could be several takes, and the show would be edited, so unless they hear the words' cut', they should continue. Each couple practiced a question and response with Brett before they broke for a lunch break.

"Wow, this is taking longer than I expected. I thought we'd already be filming," Callie announced as they were lined up at the food services table making plates. The six-foot table held platters of deli sandwiches, salad, chips, and cookies. Bottles of water were in a cooler at the end of the table. She turned to Nick beside her. "Do you think this is going to go later than five o'clock? I have to pick up my son no later than six."

Callie was the only participant that had a child. Her son, Aidan, was ten years old. They had learned about him on the first show when Callie explained how she and John had met. A little over a year ago, John walked into the law firm where Callie was a paralegal. He had an appointment with an attorney when he was introduced to Callie. After a few more meetings, he finally asked her out. She was hesitant to accept having recently divorced and was putting all her energy into her job and raising Aidan.

Aidan's dad was around often, picking up Aidan for time with him. They had what seemed to be an amicable divorce, but it turned out he was responsible for the demise of Callie and John's fledgling relationship. Callie had given John her cell number after their initial date. The next day her ex-husband had been over to pick up Aidan for the day. When John called that day, her ex-husband had answered her phone while Callie was in the shower, and never passed the message on. Furthermore, her ex had deleted John's number and blocked it. Callie assumed John was no longer interested and didn't pursue it. When John hadn't heard back from Callie, he tried to call her several times, leaving messages. Eventually, after not hearing from her in weeks, he took the hint he'd been ghosted and stopped trying to contact her. Callie had no idea in her voicemail there was a "blocked messages" folder where John's messages waited.

Six months ago John heard about the show listening to the morning radio and had happened to drive by the law firm at the very moment the advertisement asking for participants played. To him, it seemed to be a sign that he should do something out of the ordinary. At his next stop, he picked up his phone and called the show.

Nick said, "No need to worry. We will get you out of here at five. We'll pick up tomorrow wherever we leave off today."

Relieved, Callie thanked Nick.

The other couple, Hattie and Saul, was the youngest on the show. Hattie and Saul dated through their senior year at Emory University. After graduation, Hattie moved to New York to pursue her MBA while

Saul moved to California to work in Silicon Valley. The distance, school, and their workload prevented them from maintaining the relationship. They had come to agree they should see other people. Two years later, neither had found another love. Hattie heard about the show and decided to go for it.

As the four couples and Brett ate lunch seated together, Anna asked Cynthia how she and Mike met.

"I was out with my girlfriends at a bar in Boston when this tall, sexy man walked over and started chatting me up. It didn't take long for me to realize he'd had a couple of drinks, so when he asked me for my number, I said, 'if you can remember my number, call me tomorrow.' I gave him the number just before my girlfriends and I left. I thought he was cute but didn't think he'd remember. I assumed I'd never hear from him again. Well, he called me the next day. I was impressed that he had remembered my number, considering how much, I thought, he'd had to drink. After many dates, he finally told me how he remembered."

Mike continued the story, "I knew there was no way I'd remember the number. As soon as she was out of sight, I asked the bartender for a pen and wrote her name and number on my hand."

Laughter rose from the table. Brett excused himself from the table and said, "We'll start in fifteen minutes."

"He's going to go floss," Nick whispered to Anna. "Trick of the trade. Karen will remind us when we go back to makeup for touchups." Karen was the makeup artist who worked on Nick, Anna, and Brett that morning.

"Should we go then?"

"If you're done, we can head that way."

Nick and Anna returned to makeup, where Karen handed them floss and directed them back to chairs for touching up. The other couples soon joined them, and after fifteen minutes, the group was back on the set ready to film.

Anna's skin glistened under the bright set lights. She wiped her palms on her slacks and placed them on the arms of the chair, taking slow deep yoga breaths.

"You ok?" Nick put his hand on hers.

"Yeah, just trying to get centered." Nick held Anna's hand while Brett spoke to the camera introducing the show. After the filming of the couples completed, Brett would also film commercials for the show and specifically for the final episode, which would air two weeks after the last episode.

As the first couple on episode one, Cynthia and Mike started off this final episode. Brett introduced everyone to the camera then turned to Cynthia and Mike to ask what happened after the first episode taping.

"After Mike and I agreed to give us another shot, we headed to Amsterdam for a river cruise through Switzerland and Germany," Cynthia explained to Brett. "We were able to catch up and talk about what got us to where we are and how we see ourselves as a couple. Mike admitted on the show that he had a preconceived notion of what marriage was, and while we had our time away together, we were able to talk about what *our* marriage would look like. That every marriage is not the same, it will be what we want it to be."

"Have you two figured out where you'll settle? Mike is currently living in Chicago, and you're in Los Angeles, correct?" Brett filled the audience in on the detail that Mike and Cynthia live two thousand miles apart.

Mike answered, "I work for an online retail company with locations across the country. I'm hoping to transfer to California."

"Cynthia is an important part of our team here. We wish you and Mike the best. And we want an invitation to the future wedding." Brett winked at them then looked into the camera to say they'd be back to speak with Hattie and Saul.

"Cut," one of the crew yelled. The room immediately filled with the buzzing of multiple conversations.

"Nick," Callie looked to him, "If Hattie and Saul are next, we won't go on today."

"Most likely, no," Nick looked at his watch. "Looks like we'll get Hattie and Saul in today and then we'll all be free to go home for the night and be back here by eight tomorrow."

"Ok." Callie nodded. John leaned over and whispered in her ear, bringing a smile to her face.

"I'd like to know what he just said," Anna spoke softly to Nick, "that made her turn to mush."

"Give me your ear, and I'll do the same," Nick leaned toward Anna.

She shooed him away. "Our makeup will get ruined. Be good."

Nick leaned back in his chair as the director counted down to filming. The second camera assistant snapped the slate, and Brett spoke into the camera again.

Hattie beamed at Saul as Brett briefly retold what we learned during episode one about the couple.

"Hattie and Saul, you live on opposite sides of the country, too. Saul is in California, and Hattie still lives on the east coast. What happened after the show? Have you made any plans regarding your relationship?"

Saul fielded this question. "When I was asked to be on the show and told how many days I needed to be available, I put in for a two-week vacation at work. Hattie had only taken a week to be on the show, so when we left Santorini I stayed with Hattie in New York City for a week." Saul looked at Hattie as he said, "We decided to look for work in Atlanta."

"We both loved our time in Atlanta while we were in school," Hattie added, "and it's an area we are familiar with. Until then, we will visit each other as much as we can, long weekends, holidays. As it is, I have an interview in Atlanta next week. Fingers crossed," she added raising her hand with fingers crossed.

Saul took Hattie's hand in his. "Hattie," he spoke her name so she would look at him. "I didn't tell you that last week I accepted a job at an investment company in Atlanta. I'll be moving there next month."

Hattie's mouth hung open. "I can't believe it."

"I wanted to surprise you. I hope you're not upset."

"Upset? I'm stunned," a huge smile spread across Hattie's face, "and thrilled!" She hugged Saul from her chair. "I thought it would take forever." Sitting back in her chair, she looked over at Brett. "Now our visits will be a shorter flight from New York to Atlanta. That is until I get an offer." Hattie's tight brown curls bounced as she looked back at Saul.

"I hope you'll consider moving to Atlanta next month, even without a job offer." Saul got out of his chair and down on one knee as he pulled a small velvet box from his suit jacket pocket. "Hattie, I was a miserable mess without you in my life. I love you. I promise to live every day trying to make you as happy as you make me. Will you marry me?"

Hattie jumped from her seat, wrapping her arms around Saul's neck and showering him with kisses, "Yes! Yes! Yes! I love you! Yes!"

Saul stood, wrapping his arms around Hattie's waist, lifting her briefly from the ground. He placed her back down gently, and they took their seats still holding hands.

"You didn't even see the ring." Saul opened the box. He removed the delicate sapphire and diamond ring from its velvety home and slid it on Hattie's finger.

"Oh, my…." Her eyes started to shimmer. "It's beautiful. It fits perfectly. How did you get the right size?"

"When we were in New York, I took one of the silver bands you wear."

"Very sneaky," Hattie leaned over and planted a kiss on his cheek.

Brett interrupted, "Well, there's another wedding invitation we expect to get in the mail. Congratulations, Hattie and Saul. Good luck with your interview next week, Hattie." Brett spoke to the camera, and then a crewmember yelled, "Cut" again.

Immediately everyone gathered around Hattie and Saul congratulating their engagement and Saul on his new job.

Steven stepped into the group offering his congratulations and then reminded everyone to be back tomorrow for eight a.m.

Everyone dispersed quickly, wanting to take advantage of beating the rush hour traffic.

In the parking garage, Nick held the passenger door open for Anna. After she was seated he jogged around to the driver's door. Nick sat behind the steering wheel and started the car. Anna adjusted the air vents as she asked, "Nick, if everything was on the teleprompter, did Hattie know Saul was going to propose?"

Nick cleared his throat. "No, that part was left off. He ran it by Steven and I a few days ago, and we agreed to keep it a surprise."

"That was quite a surprise for all of us. Very sweet." Anna placed her hand on Nick's thigh as he navigated out of the garage. When they got to the main street, Anna asked if they could make a quick stop before heading to dinner. Nick pulled into a parking space near CVS so Anna could pick up some antacids. She complained her stomach was still giving her trouble. While Anna went inside the store, Nick waited in the car and called Steven. He wanted to make sure every-thing was all set for the next day. Anna got back in the car and popped some Tums while she waited for Nick to finish the phone call. "Say hello to Steven for me." She could tell immediately with whom he was speaking from his relaxed tone.

Nick finished his call, and they decided to have sushi for dinner and stopped at a Japanese restaurant close to Santa Monica. Once they were seated at a small table, Nick asked, "Still not feeling great, huh?"

"The Tums help. I wish we could have gone first. Then the anticipation would be over, and I could enjoy watching the other couples. Why do we have to be last?" Anna practically whined the question.

"Sorry, babe. Since we've got all the social media at-tention, we'll be last to keep the viewers watching."

"Right. I know it makes sense for us to be last, it's that my nerves can barely handle it."

The server took their order and left them with a pot of tea. Nick poured two cups. Anna blew gently on her drink and sipped. "I think I'll take a bath tonight to try to relax."

"Just remember everything will be on the tele-prompter, so you have nothing to worry about."

"Mmmhmm," was her only response.

They ate sushi and drank tea while discussing plans for getting back to a regular routine. Nick mentioned he and Steven would be writing for a new detect-ive series they planned to pitch at the end of July. That gave him a small window in August to take a vacation if she was up for it. They also looked forward to watching the aired episodes of True Loves, which would start in a couple of months and end in November. They would see the final episode just before Thanksgiving. They talked about possibly going away for that weekend.

When they got home, they headed up to the master bedroom to change, Nick into sweats and Anna to get ready for a bath. Before Anna headed into the bathroom, Nick put his hands on her waist, dipping his head to kiss her. She let the kiss linger a moment then snuggled into Nick. He tugged at the belt of her robe and slid his hands inside, causing her to shiver at his touch. Nick deepened the kiss while running his fingertips down her hips, pulling her closer to feel his erection against her stomach. She made enough space between them to run her hand up the length of him over the soft cotton pants. She moved her hands to the hem of his shirt and pulled it over his head. Freed of his shirt, he parted her robe fully while sucking and nibbling Anna's lip. His hands guided her hips, backing Anna up until she bumped against the closed bathroom door. He broke the connection of their mouths and tasted her breasts. Giving them each attention, swirling his tongue around each nipple with a gentle suck then kissing his way back to her neck. He let one hand roam south until he felt dampness between her legs. Anna pushed at his sweatpants until she could grasp his warm flesh. He used one hand to place her leg around his hip as he picked her up around the waist with the other. In one swift motion, he lowered her onto him, eliciting a moan of pleasure from her. She wrapped her other leg around his waist and bucked her hips to meet him again and again. As her climax started to build, she was thrown off balance when Nick tightened his grip around her and walked them over to the bed. He placed her down gently, not losing their connection. With her at the edge of the bed, he pushed into her slowly. "Faster, Nick," Anna pleaded. He didn't quicken but continued his languid pace. "You're killing me." She dug her nails into his butt, pulling him into her.

"But what a sweet death it would be," he laughed at her. "What's the rush?" He eased out of her to his tip then slid back in sharply to the hilt. She synchronized her hips to meet his thrusts. "No rush," she panted out as they found their rhythm. She tightened around him as color burst behind her eyes. Nick felt her pulsating and followed with his own release.

He kissed her neck again, his signature, and moved out of her. "Sorry about the mess. What can I do?" he asked, cleaning himself.

"You've done your part," she smirked as she grabbed tissues. "I'll clean up and get in the bath."

"I'll run it for you." Nick walked in the bathroom after Anna and turned on the hot water. "Do you want some bath salts in here?"

"No, thanks." Anna ushered him out and locked the door for privacy.

Nick put his shirt back on and went downstairs to watch TV. He fell asleep and only woke when Anna came into the room.

She turned off the TV. "Come up to bed," she said,

taking his hand. The scent of her soap reached his nose as he followed. Neither one mentioned they had a big day tomorrow.

TWENTY-NINE

"Callie, will you remind the audience what happened when you were on the first episode in Santorini?" Brett Taylor, host, gave a dazzling smile into the camera and turned his piercing blue eyes toward Callie. Callie wore the same cranberry dress she had the day before for show continuity, as did everyone. Even the makeup artists applied the same face to each couple. Callie looked over at John then back to Brett and began, "I got a call at work from the studio explaining that I was to receive an all-expense-paid trip to Santorini. I was told they couldn't tell me who requested my presence but someone, that I was important to, wanted to meet with me again. I couldn't imagine it was my ex-husband as we see each other regularly due to our shared custody of our son. I immediately thought of John. He was the only man I'd made a connection with since my divorce. I hoped he was the one. I agreed, contingent that I could make sure my son was cared for while I was away. I called my ex, David, and was relieved to find out he could take my son for the entire week. I was elated on two counts. One that my son would be with his father for the week, and two that it wasn't David who wanted me on the show. I racked my brain to imagine who else it could possibly be, and couldn't come up with anyone. John was the only one on my mind. When they told me it was time to walk down to the beach, I looked at my feet the entire time. It wasn't until I hit the sand I looked up to see John waiting for me. I have never felt so relieved and happy at once. After the taping, we spent a couple of days on the island and talked about what happened a year ago. I told him I never got his messages. As we figured out the timing, I realized my ex, David, would have picked up our son, Aidan, that day. John remembered speaking with a man and then calling the next few days. My phone went straight to voice-mail, where he left messages. I still have the same phone number, so, on a hunch, John had me look at my blocked messages folder. Sure enough, his messages were still there. I was really angry with David. When I addressed it with him, he apologized. At the time, our divorce was rather new, and he couldn't imagine another man in our son's life."

Addressing John, Brett asked, "John, have you had a chance to meet Aidan?"

"Callie and I took Aidan out for lunch and threw a football around at a nearby park." John looked at Callie. "Aidan's great. I think he had a good time. We're taking it slow."

Turning to Brett, Callie added, "I talked with Aidan

about John. I emphasized John isn't replacing his dad, but is someone important nt to me. His response was something like 'that's cool.' I think David and I worried too much how Aidan would handle either of us seeing someone. He's dealt with the divorce like a champ, so I shouldn't be surprised that he's managing my relationship with John so well."

"What's next for you two?"

"Considering we only live a couple of towns apart, we're going to continue to see each other. We don't need to make any drastic changes or uproot anyone's life. The most important thing is making sure Aidan's life doesn't change radically. He'll continue to share time with David and me. If some of his time with me is also with John, then that's great, too." Callie turned to John for any additional input.

"Just what Callie said, continue to see each other and not make any big changes for Aidan. Let him get used to me being around." John smiled at Callie.

Brett looked into the camera, "It sounds like things are off to a good start for you two. We wish you all the best on this reconnection. Next, we'll speak with the couple that has been all over social media lately, our own producer and his wife, Nick and Anna." Brett continued to look into the camera and bring the audience up to speed, "Nick and Anna's story is a little different than most of the couples who have come on True Loves; Nick and Anna are a married couple. Nick is one of the producers of the show and hosted the first episode as a favor to our assistant producer and episode one guest, Cynthia. During the taping of the first episode, Anna interrupted filming. Here's the clip." Brett paused. A clip of the video would be inserted during editing. Then he continued, "Let's find out what this was all about." Turning to Anna and Nick, he read off the teleprompter, "Anna, can you explain what you were thinking when you accused Nick of infidelity?"

Anna swallowed and took a deep breath. "I have an overactive imagination," she read off the teleprompter while appearing to look at Brett. "Nick had been spending a lot of late nights at work with his beautiful assistant producer, Cynthia. Which I misinterpreted as an affair."

"Nick, did you have an affair?" Brett looked intensely at Nick as he dropped the big question.

"Brett, this was truly a huge misunderstanding. No, I did not cheat on my wife. This job comes with a crazy schedule, and we were missing each other. A lot." Nick held Anna's hand.

"Anna, you were pretty heated when you left the set that day. How did you two reconcile afterward? We have the video of that moment here." Brett paused, and Anna waited to respond until Steven, standing next to the camera, nodded his head, giving her the signal she was clear to answer.

"Nick was able to get me a copy of the show ahead of the air date, so I was able to watch the entire episode and see that all those late nights were for work. Cynthia was trying to find her own true love, not fall in love with mine. After I came to the conclusion I was worked up for, literally, no reason, I decided to surprise Nick, who was still on the island finishing production. That scene in the pool was my attempt to get his attention before he left the island, not knowing I had arrived."

"It was pretty steamy," Brett commented. "Certainly a couple still deeply in love." Continuing to look at Nick and Anna, Brett continued his questioning, "A lot of viewers could empathize with Anna questioning Nick's fidelity. Anna, what would you have done differently if you could?"

"Oh, Brett, I asked myself that question many times. It seems so obvious now, but for some reason, at the moment, I didn't think to talk about it with Nick. I would have talked about the late nights and my feelings. How I was feeling a lack of connection with our busy schedules. Instead, I was pretending everything was okay. Maybe nothing could have changed regarding his travel and the hours he needed to put in, but the time we had together would have been different. I wouldn't have been questioning him or our relationship because I would have had the answers I needed." She looked at Nick and ad-libbed, "Maybe I should have hired a private investigator, and then I would have known everything was aboveboard."

Nick raised his eyebrows, surprised that Anna would stray from the scripted material.

"Nick, what is next for the two of you?" Brett asked the next question, not giving Nick time to respond to Anna.

"Work never slows, we're always working on the

next idea, but we do get vacation time. Our next step is to take a bona fide vacation, just the two of us. We are also hoping to start a family, if we're lucky," Nick smiled at Anna and gave her a wink. "We want to get back to our life, concentrating on not taking each other for granted and continuing to treasure each other and our relationship."

Before Brett could read off the teleprompter to end the show, Anna spoke up. "Brett, I want to correct something Nick just said." Brett just smiled, waiting to see where she was going with another impromptu addition of verbiage. "Nick said we are hoping to start a family." Nick looked over at Anna with a furrowed brow. "He meant to say we have started a family." She placed her hand on her stomach.

It took Nick a full three seconds to digest what Anna said, a huge smile spread across his face. "Really?"

"Yes, really."

Nick picked up Anna's hand and kissed it. "Well, this is one hell of a way to tell me!" Anna closed her smile over her teeth, but couldn't stop the grin that ate up the bottom half of her face. Nick continued to shake his head in disbelief, rubbing her hand in slow rhythmic circles, his smile as wide as Anna's.

Brett took that as a cue to speak. "Congratulations, Anna and Nick! Wow! Thank you for sharing that with us today." Turning to the camera, he said, "That's our finale! Two engagements and a pregnancy! We'll keep you posted on our couples' lives with our social media app, so check in daily for updates."

Someone yelled, "Cut!" and everyone was out of their seats crowding around Nick and Anna.

Nick pulled Anna from her seat and hugged her gently, kissing her hair. He kept one protective arm around her as they accepted congratulations from the other couples.

Steven approached and patted Nick on the shoulder. "Congratulations. Looks like you'll be extra busy in nine months."

To the group, he said, "You are all free to go today. We'll be in touch."

Turning back to Nick and Anna, he embraced Anna and added, "I think that ending may just have guaranteed us another season."

"That's not my main concern at the moment," Nick looked down at Anna, "I can't decide if I'm more shocked that you're pregnant or that you told about a million other people. What made you decide to announce that here?"

"I figured our life was already on display, why not give the viewers something juicy?"

"You are ridiculous! I love you." Nick kissed her again. Turning to Steven, "I'll catch you tomorrow. Right now, I'm taking my pregnant wife home."

They said their goodbyes and headed to the parking garage. As they turned out of the garage, Nick asked, "How long have you known? Is that what all the bellyaches were about?"

"I hope you won't be too upset. I just took the test last night."

"What?! Seriously?"

"Yes. When we stopped for the antacids, I picked up a pregnancy test. The stomachaches are tied to my anxiety; it's too soon for morning sickness. Now that the taping is over, I feel one hundred percent better." She inhaled and exhaled deeply enjoying the lack of queasiness that had plagued her. "I was expecting to start my period a week ago, but with everything going on, I hadn't thought about it until yesterday morning. Anxiety can delay it and I typically wouldn't think twice about being late, but since we haven't been using protection, I decided to check, just in case. Last night before I got in the tub, I took the pregnancy test. I almost told you last night but decided it would be more exciting to do it at the end of the show. I knew you would be mentioning starting a family, thanks to the prewritten responses." Anna smiled smugly.

"Our life is going to get a lot busier in…how far along are you?"

"It's only a few weeks. I'll call to make an appointment with my doctor."

"Well, then, in roughly nine months, our lives will be even busier, as Steven aptly mentioned at the studio. We better plan that vacation soon. Where do you want to go?" Nick steered the car onto Route 10, heading back toward Santa Monica.

"Oh, I don't really care, as long as we're together. We could just hang out at home."

"You don't want to go on a cruise like Cynthia and Mike did? Or that resort in Bellagio?"

"I guess I'm already feeling ready to, what do they

say about pregnant women, I'm ready to nest." She placed her hand in Nick's. "If we get away somewhere, great. If not, we'll always have Santorini."

THE END

ABOUT THE AUTHOR

Danielle Fluehr

Danielle lives in Rhode Island with her husband and two children. Fascinated by human psychology and how experiences shape the ability to trust and love, Danielle loves love and believes the best feeling in the world is being in  love and having that love returned. If you are fortunate enough to find it, enjoy those fleeting moments that may turn into a lifetime.

This is her first work of romantic contemporary fiction. She is currently writing a suspense novel and contemplating writing the stories of Beth and Drew, Lauren and Mark, or the prequel for Anna and Nick.

www.ingramcontent.com/pod-product-compliance
Lightning Source LLC
Chambersburg PA
CBHW020909160726
47993CB00005B/1893